Out of Silence

"Inspired by true events"

Ruby Monroe

authorHOUSE

AuthorHouse™
1663 Liberty Drive
Bloomington, IN 47403
www.authorhouse.com
Phone: 1 (800) 839-8640

© 2017 Ruby Monroe. All rights reserved.

No part of this book may be reproduced, stored in a retrieval system, or transmitted by any means without the written permission of the author.

Published by AuthorHouse 11/06/2017

ISBN: 978-1-5462-1568-4 (sc)
ISBN: 978-1-5462-1566-0 (hc)
ISBN: 978-1-5462-1567-7 (e)

Library of Congress Control Number: 2017917033

Print information available on the last page.

Any people depicted in stock imagery provided by Thinkstock are models, and such images are being used for illustrative purposes only. Certain stock imagery © Thinkstock.

This book is printed on acid-free paper.

Because of the dynamic nature of the Internet, any web addresses or links contained in this book may have changed since publication and may no longer be valid. The views expressed in this work are solely those of the author and do not necessarily reflect the views of the publisher, and the publisher hereby disclaims any responsibility for them.

Contents

Chapter 1	1966	1
Chapter 2	Back to the Beginning: 1955	11
Chapter 3	September 1955	18
Chapter 4	Fall 1955	20
Chapter 5	Ruby at Age 11	22
Chapter 6	Unwanted News	25
Chapter 7	A Not So Merry Christmas	33
Chapter 8	Sharing Family Secrets	35
Chapter 9	1956 Brings New Beginnings	37
Chapter 10	New Adventure: March 1956	39
Chapter 11	Arrival of a Bundle of Joy	44
Chapter 12	The Next Phase: June 1957	47
Chapter 13	Tenth Wedding Anniversary, January 13 1966	52
Chapter 14	Married Fourteen Years Now	59
Chapter 15	1971: Married for Fifteen Years	62
Chapter 16	1972: Married Sixteen Years	65
Chapter 17	1973: Finally Proof	69
Chapter 18	1976: Married Twenty Years	73
Chapter 19	Early May 1976: The Turning Point	75
Chapter 20	1978: Changes and Motivation	77
Chapter 21	1978: Plans Coming Together—or Disrupted?	80
Chapter 22	1978: Another Problem	91
Chapter 23	1978: Married Twenty-Two Years	95
Chapter 24	1978 – Late Summer	99
Chapter 25	1979: Moving Day	104
Chapter 26	1979 Continued	113
Chapter 27	Life Now A New Normal	117
Chapter 28	January 1979	119

Chapter 29	Summer 1979	122
Chapter 30	Summer 1979 Cont'd	125
Chapter 31	1980: On the Move Again	128
Chapter 32	1980: Moving On	132
Chapter 33	Pushed Out	135
Chapter 34	1982: A New Chapter	138
Chapter 35		141
Chapter 36	A New Slant on Recruitment	145
Chapter 37	California—Here Comes Ruby	148
Chapter 38		155
Chapter 39	1981: More Changes	157
Chapter 40	Life Changing Decision	159

Epilogue ... 163

Chapter 1

1966

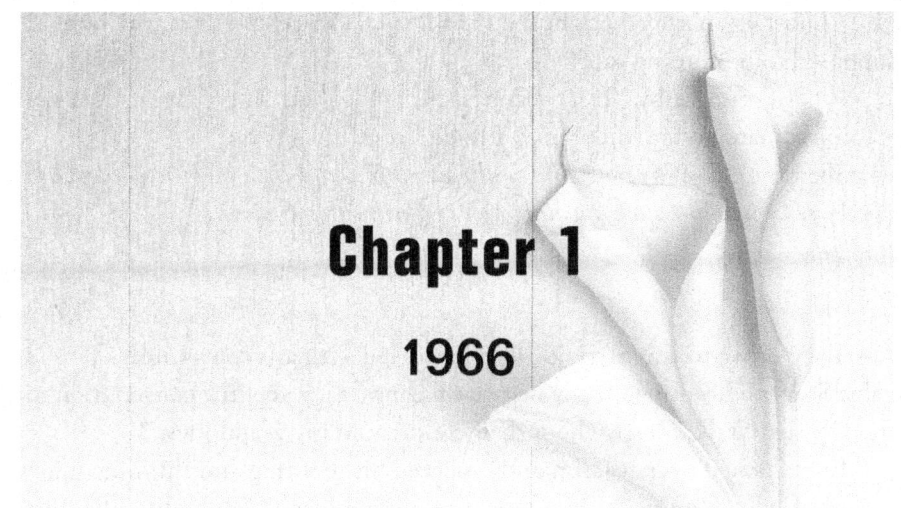

A naked, almost anorexic image in the full-length mirror stared back at a shocked Ruby. She dragged her hands down the sides of her skeletal figure and over ribs and bony hips that seemed to push through her skin. Only now did she realize how very thin her body had become. The dress she chose hung more loosely than it was ever meant to. She'd lost her appetite. Eating was just not a priority these days. She slowly walked back to the closet and selected a dress with a fuller skirt and ruffles that concealed her frame.

Tears gathered when she saw her gaunt face and sunken eyes reflected in her vanity mirror. She leaned in for a closer look. It would take more makeup than ever to transform her face and cover the discoloration of older bruises. Her gray-hued skin and the bags under her sad, deep-set blue eyes told her story. Everyone used to admire her inner glow; where had it gone? She tugged at her shoulder-length blonde hair and pulled it forward to cover the bruises on her neck and hide her emaciated face. Tears pooled in eyes that had once twinkled with happiness.

Earlier that week, Ruby had been busy cooking dinner when her husband, Jason, interrupted to announce in an unusually upbeat tone, "Hey, Ruby. Lloyd, the new guy at work—I don't think you've met him—is having a house party this Saturday. We're invited along with several of the guys from our department. I think you've met some of them at other functions. I would really like to go. It's actually sort of important to me."

She was so lost in thought, trying to figure out how she felt about going to an office party, that she didn't realize that he had paused, waiting for her reaction to the invitation.

Almost as an afterthought, he continued, "Oh yeah. Jackie, my boss, is supposed to be coming too."

"Okay," said Ruby. "If it means that much to you, I agree we should go. It's kind of late notice, though, so I hope I can find a sitter."

She thought, *Why not? This will please him, and then he'll be happy with me. It seems like I'm always walking on eggshells around him.*

They drove to the party in their flashy red Camaro convertible—Jason's baby. So as not to bring up any negative feelings, they kept the conversation to friendly small talk, mostly about their children: Matt, 9, and Joey, 3.

Ruby looked over at Jason and observed his receding and thinning gray-peppered hair. He was heavier now, too, with a small paunch he called his beer belly. She would never have mentioned this to him, as he would first deny it and then be furious. She wondered how their once happy marriage had become such a nightmare. How *did* it happen?

"Ruby, pay attention. I'm talking to you." Jason poked her shoulder with his index finger.

She winced and slightly recoiled at the sharp jab. "What? I'm sorry. I was deep in thought." She managed a little smile. The last thing she wanted to do was annoy him so early in the evening.

"I said we're here," Jason declared with that harsh, controlling tone.

She knew this evening would be good only if she was submissive. "You seem to be really excited about going to this party with your work buddies," she offered in a feigned happy voice. Jason had not been in such high spirits for quite some time. This was an odd but pleasant change.

The house where the party took place was in a recently built cookie-cutter subdivision of two-story brick attached homes. Newly planted trees lined the streets. Lawns had recently been sodded, but sidewalks were not yet in place. The house was one of many in this new, large family-oriented neighbourhood.

Lloyd—a tall, thin, fair-haired and light-skinned fella—and Susan, his wife, also of Scandinavian heritage, were their host and hostess. Lloyd wrapped his arm around Susan, ending at her narrow waist just below her breasts. They seemed quite comfortable with each other. Susan looked up at Lloyd and winked. This caring gesture caused Ruby to feel a flash of envy sweep over her body.

"Lloyd, Susan, this is my wife, Ruby," Jason said.

Smiling, Susan greeted them with an extended hand. "Hello. We're so glad you guys came."

"Nice to finally meet you, Ruby," Lloyd offered. "Here—let me take your coats."

"Thank you," said Ruby. As they entered the house, Ruby exclaimed, "Susan, you have a lovely home." She immediately liked the new couple.

Ruby remembered when Jason was attentive, just like Lloyd. When friends came over for drinks and dinner, he would look at her, give her a quick hug and say, "My lovely wife deserves nothing but the best." Ruby mentally shook herself out of this regressive thought process, as it would surely spoil their big night out.

Susan directed them to the family room, where the partygoers had gathered. Jason stopped to chat with a coworker.

When they entered the family room, Ruby was immediately impressed with the decor. She asked, "Susan, are you the decorator?"

"Guilty," Susan said with a smile and a nod.

"Your home feels calm and inviting. It feels very comfortable." Ruby liked both the contemporary style and the palette of autumn colors, mostly beige and brown, with burnt orange and olive green as accents.

"Thank you, Ruby."

"Neat trick, the aroma of freshly baked appetizers and desserts. The first whiff tickled my nose."

"I do my best. Let me introduce you to Sarah, a good friend of mine."

"Thanks."

"Excuse me, Sarah. I'd like to introduce you to Ruby, Jason's wife. Would you mind introducing her to a few folks?"

"Sure, Susan." Sarah walked Ruby to a small group of Susan's neighbours and introduced her.

"There's the doorbell again. Gotta go," Susan said over her shoulder as she left to continue her hostess duties.

Ruby chatted for a while with the group and then chose to move on. She studied the crowd and counted about thirty people already at the party. Everyone was drinking, munching on snacks, laughing and chatting. Ruby was determined to show Jason that she could have a good time. She slowly crept out of her shell.

She approached a female about her age and said, "Hello, I'm Ruby—Ruby Monroe." They juggled their beverages to shake hands. Ruby smiled to herself. She was out.

"Hi, I'm Janice. I work for Jason in accounting," the woman said. "It's nice to finally meet you, Ruby."

"Thanks." Ruby searched for a common topic and then decided to ask, "Do you have children?"

"Yes, a beautiful 1-year-old boy, Andrew." Janice just happened to be wearing a charm bracelet that held a photo of Andrew. "Look—isn't he a cutie?"

"He certainly is. What a great age he's at. I'm sure you would prefer to be at home with him."

"I would, but we do what we can to spend quality time with him."

Comfortable with the conversation, Ruby asked, "You probably know we have two boys, Matt and Joey."

"I hear they're a handful. I think one is all I want for now." Janice smiled to welcome another female to their group. "Hi, Patty. Have you met Ruby, Jason's wife?"

"No. Hello, Ruby. Good to meet you."

Cautiously, Ruby continued her participation in the now three-way conversation. To avoid sharing details of her life, she asked the questions. The happy party atmosphere made her feel more like her old self. Secretly, she wished they socialized more often.

Throughout the evening, as Ruby got bolder, she interjected herself into several discussions and circulated among the clusters of people. Health and the issues of raising children were the main topics. Ruby was comfortable with these subjects. Oddly, she felt like she belonged. She was happy that they had come to the party and confident that she did the right thing by accompanying Jason.

She wondered why a few of the women who spoke to her didn't make eye contact, and some others completely avoided her. Why? She wondered if she had food or lipstick on her teeth and they just didn't know how to tell her. Ruby excused herself and made her way to the powder room. She leaned in to have a closer look in the mirror and examined her teeth and makeup. There was no evidence of food or misplaced lipstick. The bruises were still hidden, too. *Odd…*

It was around this time that she noticed Jason was no longer in the family room with the other guests. It was getting late. Ruby had told their sitter they would be home by midnight, and it was already after eleven thirty. She smiled, excused herself from the group and wandered away to look for Jason.

Unable to find him, Ruby approached the hostess, with whom she had seen Jason speaking earlier. "Excuse me, Susan. Have you seen Jason? It's getting late, and our sitter needs to be home by twelve."

Susan hesitated slightly, frowned and then pursed her lips trying to remember when it was that she had last seen him and which way he was headed. "Yes," she said. Her face lit up. "Yes, I saw Jason going upstairs about twenty minutes ago. He may not still be there, but feel free to check."

Ruby smiled graciously, thanked Susan and made her way to the stairs. *Why was he upstairs when all of the other partygoers were on the main level?* she wondered.

When she reached the top stair, to her disbelief, she saw Jason across the hall and inside one of the bedrooms. He was passionately kissing a well-developed youngish blonde woman. Their clothing had become dishevelled and unbuttoned. Their hands were busy exploring intimate parts of each other's body. It stung as if Jason had just slapped her across the face.

Ruby's first thought was to retreat, run back downstairs and hide like an abused animal. But no! Not this time. She would not flee. She would stand her ground. Normally, she wouldn't confront Jason, because she knew the hell that would rain down upon her. Was it jealousy or possessiveness? Her motivation was not immediately evident to her. She didn't know why, but for some reason, she was compelled to stop the scene that distressed her. Ruby's insides were quivering with anger as she cautiously but deliberately strode over to the entwined bodies.

She tugged on her husband's sleeve and demanded, "Jason, what are you doing?"

He turned and gave Ruby a piercing look that would strip paint from a wall. He disentangled himself from the girl, turned and said, "I'm sorry, Jackie, but my rude wife just doesn't understand how things go at these parties."

He's apologizing to that woman, not me? This is so humiliating. I'm so embarrassed.

Jason adjusted his clothing and tucked his shirt into his trousers. He grabbed Ruby tightly by her forearm and forcibly guided her down the stairs. It didn't matter to him that this roughness caused her to stumble several times.

"Jason, you're hurting my arm. Let go," she pleaded.

He glared at her and then between gritted teeth sneered and mumbled, "Why do you always embarrass me? You wonder why I don't take you anywhere. Now, because of you, we need to get out of here. I'm mortified by your behaviour."

Guests within earshot of this scene purposely looked away to avoid making eye contact or getting involved. *Oh my God! They all knew. Wow.*

In the car, Jason's mood went from bad to worse. He furiously waved his hands around much too close to her. She feared his hand or fist would make contact. His face twisted with anger, almost touching hers. She smelled the liquor. He jabbed his index finger into her shoulder as if he intended to stab her with it. Angrily, he screamed, "I could kill you! Why do you humiliate me in front of my work friends? Your mother was right. You're a stupid bitch."

When she finally stopped shaking and gained control of her fear, she reminded herself to not share her feelings with him. She had to remember that sharing her inner thoughts would always come back to haunt her. He frequently used her guarded secrets against her.

"I take you out. I try to be nice to you. And again you are an embarrassment. You wonder why I don't take you anywhere. Well, this is exactly why."

They had been driving in silence for a short while when she realized that Jason was too drunk to be driving. Her heart pounded, and the waking of some old familiar spasms and cramps in her belly added to her panic. He had turned onto the main drag, but into the lane headed in the wrong direction.

Conscious of the retribution she knew would be inflicted on her for criticizing his driving, she screamed, "Jason, look! Please! Stop now!" She clutched his arm and pointed to the oncoming headlights.

He angrily brushed her hand off his arm. "Don't tell me how to drive, you useless piece of shit. I don't know why I put up with you."

Frantic, again, she tried to get his attention. Ruby grabbed the steering wheel. Jason violently swatted her hand, swearing at her. "Don't you ever do that again! I'm driving. Keep your hands off the damn steering wheel."

"But you're not listening!" She screamed louder. "Jason, stop. We need to get off this road. Look at the headlights. They're coming right at us." She had no choice but to scream again even louder than before, *"Jason. Stop the car. Now!* You're driving in the wrong direction. Those vehicles are going to kill us. They're approaching us way too fast." Her heart was pounding as if it was trying to escape from her chest. She could feel adrenaline racing through her veins. Pointing with a nervous hand to the vehicles' bright lights that were quickly approaching them, she gasped in horror.

Shocked by the impending danger, Jason seemed to quickly sober up. She watched his attempt to avoid a collision with the oncoming vehicles. He tried to make a U-turn toward the middle of the road.

"Oh my God, Jason. You can't turn here! The median is too high," she exclaimed. "We're going to die! You're going to kill us. What are you going to do? Think of something, fast!"

One of the oncoming vehicles blinded them with its bright headlights. She held her breath and opened her mouth to scream, but there was no sound. The driver blasted his horn as he sped past.

Several more cars were approaching. Jason slammed his foot down hard on the gas pedal and then suddenly increased the speed, which jolted them backward. At the last second, he turned into a plaza parking area. Now the threatening vehicles were only lights whizzing past in their rear-view mirror. A huge sigh of relief filled their vehicle.

Then Jason resumed his verbal abuse. "You see what you made me do? You're such a bitch. I don't know why I put up with you and your bullshit. Your nagging almost caused a fatal accident."

"Why are you blaming me? You're the one who turned into the wrong lane, not me." Ruby knew from past experience she would pay dearly for defending herself.

When they arrived home, he stayed civil until the sitter left.

Once alone, Ruby asked, "Was that woman you were kissing your boss? Are you having an affair? Tell me. What's going on here?"

He refused to discuss his indiscretion. "It's none of your damn business. If you weren't so incapable of having good sex, I wouldn't need to look elsewhere."

"You know that's not true. Why would you say that?" she retorted. "True, I don't feel like having sex with you when you make out with one of your coworkers. Answer me, was that woman Jackie your new boss?"

"What does it matter? You'll never see her again."

"So that's who she is, your boss. How l—"

"You're asking for trouble. Just shut up!" He glared at her with his most frightening look.

"Why not tell me?" she pushed.

"None of you're bus—"

"How long have you been screwing her?"

"My business is my busi—"

"As usual, you're thinking with the wrong part of your body."

This comment angered him beyond any past episodes of brutality. He grabbed her hair and pulled her head back with such force that he knocked her off her feet. She groaned when her knees slammed onto the floor.

"Let go, Jason, stop. Stop. Please stop." She felt the most intense pain, plus a burning sensation on her scalp like it was on fire. Her hands desperately tried to hold her hair to her head. She worried that he might actually pull her hair out by the roots.

She stopped screaming and bit her lip instead. She feared her cries would wake up the children. *I hope they didn't hear me. It would be just too horrifying for them to see their mommy suffering like this.*

Dizzy and shaken, she pleaded, "Jason, let go. You're hurting me. Please stop. I will do better. I promise."

He let go of her hair only to tightly grip her right arm. He hauled her to her feet and pummelled her body with the clenched fist of his other hand. His face was so close she felt a wet spray on her face.

"Stop hitting me! Please don't hit me again. Just tell me what you want me to do," she pleaded. "I'm so sorry that I embarrassed you in front of your friends. I'm really sorry that I pried. I promise I'll never do that again."

"You're damn right you won't, because I'll never take you out again, *ever*. I should put all of us out of our misery."

Oh my God. He's going to kill us all just like he's threatened to so many times.

It felt like her whole body was screaming with pain. *I'm so tired of being his punching bag.* Ruby wept.

Once her arm was freed, she struggled to move away from him. She bent over with her head down to stop the dizziness. She feared she would faint. *Oh! Oh! My head hurts so much.* She closed her eyes and gently supported her head in her hands just because it made her feel better. *Maybe I should go to the hospital and get checked out? No, no, what am I thinking? I can't do that. He'll be really angry if I even suggest telling anyone or talk about getting help.*

He hurled another barrage of deprecating warnings and promises of the physical beatings and psychological torture in store for her if she ever crossed him again. He raised his blood-covered fist and threatened to punch her once more. She jerked back.

He sneered, "I'm tired of you humiliating me in front of my friends. You're such a drag. Why did I get stuck with you? You probably got yourself pregnant on purpose just to trap me."

Ruby cowered beside a bookcase, wishing she was invisible to him.

"I know how malicious you can be. If I had figured you out long ago, I wouldn't be confined like a prisoner in this useless marriage. It seems obvious to me that you were desperate to get away from your family, and no one else wanted you."

On and on it went. It never changed. Everything bad was her fault. Ruby was the prisoner in the marriage and wished she knew how to escape from her hell.

Ruby shifted left and out of Jason's reach. She quietly whispered, "I'm going to bed."

She readied for bed. Fleetingly, she peeked in the mirror at her stripped-down aching body. She gasped at the new red and purple injuries that started to appear over older yellowish bruises. *What a mess I am. No wonder he treats me like I'm nobody. This evening was entirely my fault—I shouldn't have talked back to him.* She lay on her side of the bed still as a corpse, pretending to be asleep. Tears escaped and trickled across her cheeks onto her pillow.

A few minutes later, Jason joined her in bed.

"Ruby you know that I really do love you. You're still and will always be my special lady. C'mon, let's make love." He spoke ever so softly in his sickly syrupy voice. He tried to snuggle up to her. He kissed her neck, nibbled on her ears and fondled her breasts. "I'm horny. Let's make out, okay?"

"No. Go away. Leave me alone." *It's not natural, I know, but I cringe when he comes near me. Just the thought of him touching my body right now makes my skin crawl.*

"Come on, baby. I'm so sorry. You know I'm crazy about you."

Ruby was sore, angry and mortified by the events of earlier that evening. She winced at the metallic taste of blood from her now swollen lip. "Please don't. I just want to go to sleep. Leave me alone. Don't … Jason … You're hurting me." She recoiled from the unbearably strong smell of liquor on his breath.

Ruby knew deep down that Jason had already decided he was going to have sex, come hell or high water. He forced himself on her. He was aroused by either the act of making out with the other woman or the physical abuse. She never knew which one turned him on more. Jason tried to force himself into Ruby's mouth. She buried her head in her pillow. "No, leave me alone. I'm not interested." She pushed him away.

Jason, committed to having his gratification, flipped her onto her back and selfishly drove his large aroused penis into her dry unwilling vagina. He settled for intercourse with or without her participation.

She held her breath, closed her eyes and suffered in silence. *I will not cry out. He must know how much that hurts. This pain is excruciating. It feels like he's ripping my insides apart. He always wants to control me, but this is torture.*

Ruby escaped by letting her mind drift back to a very special midnight cruise and a memorable birthday. That was such a wonderful evening—dancing cheek-to-cheek and later strolling arm-in-arm around the promenade deck. She fell head over heels in love with him that night. He was so kind and considerate, and such a gentleman. *We were gently rocked by the ship gliding through the calm waters. When the ship arrived back at our home port, we held each other, whispering sweet nothings into each other's ears. Our hearts were filled to the brim with hopes and happy thoughts. Oh so very peaceful.*

Mechanically, Jason came, removed himself and rolled over to his side of the bed. He angrily spat at her, "You're a cold fish, Ruby. I don't know why I waste my time on you."

She lay there like a discarded old rag. She felt worthless and used.

Once again, he had raped her.

Ruby yearned to be free of the monster lying next to her. *How could I have ever thought that I loved him? I hate him so much. If only he would just go away. Will I ever be free of his abuse? Why does he always make me the guilty one?*

Silently, she cried herself to sleep, wishing she was dead.

Chapter 2

Back to the Beginning: 1955

As Ruby drove to work the next day, "Rock Around the Clock" blasted from the radio of their 1966 Chevy. Ruby loved Bill Haley and the Comets. Singing along took her back to the fifties—and to the event that changed her life forever.

It was July 1955. Ruby's sixteenth birthday was just two weeks away.

She was a slender well-developed gal with an athletic body and firm muscles from running in competitions. Ruby was pretty, with blonde hair and blue eyes, and she was popular with her peers. Her fair complexion and full-busted body worked well with her choice of pastel colours and her hip teen style. She was mature both physically and mentally beyond her years.

Her best friend, Debbie—everyone's sweetheart—suggested that they should do something special for Ruby's memorable day. Deb had a nicely proportioned petite frame, very curly shoulder-length blond hair and the bluest of blue eyes, plus a cute mole on her right cheek just below her eye.

Deb had read in the travel section of the Saturday newspaper about the coolest midnight cruise. It took place every Saturday evening during the summer. The ship traveled to Niagara-on-the-Lake and then back, arriving in their home port of Toronto about two in the morning. Deb enthusiastically insisted that this midnight cruise would be the best and most perfect place to celebrate Ruby's sweet 16, making it unforgettable.

"Debbie, I agree, it would be amazing, but have you asked your mother yet?"

"Yes. She said if your mom agrees, she'll let me go."

"Thanks for the pressure. You know my mom. She can be difficult, and getting her permission may not happen. Cross your fingers, girl."

Ruby wrinkled up her nose as she entered the kitchen. She hated the awful smell of the overcooked cabbage that would be her dinner tonight. Her mother, Sarah, as was her habit, sat at the chrome and laminate kitchen table reading the evening edition of their local newspaper as she waited for their dinner to cook—or overcook, according to Ruby's nose.

Ruby's childhood home was built by her grandfather shortly after his family arrived in Canada from London, England, in 1906. It was a large three-story red brick house with gray wood verandas the width of the house on both the first and second floors. Three generous principle rooms took up the first floor, and there was a total of five bedrooms on the two floors above. The furnishings were old antiques, but this feature was lost on modern Ruby. The bathroom had a tub—a deep claw-footed one—was located on the second floor.

Apprehensively, Ruby approached her mother. "Mom, Debbie and I want to celebrate my birthday by going on a midnight cruise. It travels to Niagara-on-the-Lake every Saturday evening. Mom, please, can I go? *Please*?

"You're only 15," her mother said without changing her focus from the newspaper.

"We'll stay together. Don't worry. You know we're responsible."

Her mother didn't respond.

"I'll be 16 in four days. Lots of people my age go out on short trips like this. You don't need to worry. We'll be okay. *Please*," Ruby begged.

"Stop pestering me. You're both too young to be out that late by yourselves. You really don't know what can happen to innocent young girls. There are some really bad people preying on them."

"I promise you, we'll stay together. We'll go directly from the streetcar to the ship and then do the same when we get back. I promise, we won't talk to any strangers," she begged—being very careful not to mention that the ship didn't dock until 2:00 a.m.

"If you get into trouble out there, I will not be coming to your rescue," her mother warned.

Sarah was old-fashioned and very strict. She hadn't allowed Ruby to go to the evening movies or on a date, even with a group of her neighbourhood friends, until Ruby was past 13. She held a tight rein on her daughter. Often, Ruby had been told by her mother that men were bad news. After seven children, Sarah understood what men wanted and the consequences of their lust. The last three pregnancies were change-of-life babies, Ruby being one of those born after her mother was 40 years old. Ruby recognized that her mother was tired.

"Mom, please. I'll be very careful. I have money saved up, so I'll pay for the trip with my savings and the next few weeks' allowances. You know that Deb and I have been good friends for a very long time. We'll look out for each other."

Ruby continued to make her case. She could see her mother was wavering a little. Ruby knew her gray-haired mother was worn out, not all that healthy and overweight, which seemed to sap her of her energy.

Finally, Sarah looked up at Ruby. "It goes against my better judgment to let you go. I think it's not wise for you two to go by yourselves." Sarah just didn't have much fight left in her.

"Mom, please!" Ruby begged to give that little extra nudge.

"Okay … okay, go," Sarah gave in, and then deep in thought shook her head from side to side and turned her focus back to her newspaper. She continued reading as if the discussion had never taken place.

Ruby ran out the door and across the street to Debbie's house. She wanted to share the great news. Deb hardly had the front door open when Ruby shouted, "I can go! I can go! My mother said I can go! I can't believe it. My mother agreed." Ruby grinned from ear to ear as she skipped a few happy steps.

Debbie clapped her hands to her cheeks and joined Ruby, half-skipping and half-jumping for joy alongside to show her delight. "We're going to have the most amazing time."

With their mothers' permission and sufficient money saved, they booked their passage. Both were ecstatic at the prospect of a romantic interlude. The girls spent the next two weeks fantasizing about the sensational fun they were going to have aboard ship.

It seemed like it took forever, but their special Saturday finally arrived—and none too soon, either. They had nearly worn themselves out with stories of fairy tale adventures; meeting their Prince Charming; and anticipating what could be the most incredible evening.

Once onboard the small cruise ship, they took a little tour. The glass-enclosed main deck included a full-service dining room with white tablecloths, fine china and sterling silver cutlery. Waiters and a maître d', all in spiffy white uniforms, waited to serve.

"This is too rich for us," Ruby admitted. "Let's get out of here."

Moving on, they found their way to the second deck, where they stopped at the railing and watched their departure. The ship chugged as it left the shore, and slowly the city's skyline of multi-storey buildings shrunk and faded from view.

It was a beautiful warm July evening. The fresh smell of the summer lake brought back memories of being at the cottage Ruby's parents owned—a traditional rustic cabin on a large lake about an hour north of the city. Most summers her mother, brothers and sisters spent weeks on end there until school resumed. Watersports, BBQs and the smoky smell of late-night bonfires that got stuck in her nostrils were among Ruby's favourite memories.

The cruise ship, now at full speed, glided over the smooth lake. The full moon reflected off the glass-like water. The deck on this level consisted of a highly polished dance floor and a raised stage area that held speakers and amplifiers for the musicians that would serenade the dancers. Loud music blasted from the dance band, bounced off the water and disappeared into the night. The dancers were happily dreaming of possibilities and making new friends.

Ruby spotted a great-looking guy leaning against the railing that circled the room. He casually sipped from a bottle of Red Cap beer. "Debbie, look at that hunk across the room in the white shirt and black pants. I wouldn't mind dating him. He's *so* handsome."

The moment she laid eyes on Jason, Ruby knew she would marry him. He was gorgeous like a movie star.

Jason spotted Ruby at about the same time. He sauntered indirectly across the dance floor toward her. She blushed and accepted his invitation to dance. Her heart pounded when their sweaty hands touched.

They flirted, danced, talked and danced some more. They were most definitely attracted to each other. His sensual cologne drew her closer to him. She became intoxicated with his irresistible fragrance.

He was three years older than Ruby. At 19 years of age, he was also more experienced, and she loved that about him. His Italian features, coloring and slim body sealed the deal for her. He had large brown eyes and dark brown hair that he combed back and held in place with Brilliantine. Jason had a cute little dimple in the middle of his chin that reminded her of her heartthrob, the movie star Robert Mitchum.

Jason obviously said all of the right things to Ruby. They stole kisses, and he sneaked quick touches of her breasts in the dark shadows on deck. By the end of the evening, Ruby and Jason were enthralled with each other. Young love was wonderful. They stood with arms wrapped around each other at the deck railing and watched as the night-lit city sprouted before their eyes. Just before they docked, he asked for her phone number. Excitedly, she complied, hoping to hear from him soon—very soon. Ruby was certain she was in love like only a 16-year-old could be.

She floated on cloud nine for days after the cruise. Her emotions ran the gamut of excitement, anticipation and then fear that Jason would never call. Ruby and Debbie frequently giggled and planned what she should say when and if Jason finally telephoned her. Many hours were spent rehashing the events of that blissful night on their wonderfully romantic cruise. She so wanted to contact him, but he hadn't given her his number.

Her summer job as a telephone operator for the local phone company helped keep her mind busy. She was a good student who liked school. She looked forward to pursuing a higher education and maybe someday having a job as a nurse. That was her vision of a perfect life.

It had been a torturous two weeks of waiting. She ran for the hallway phone every time it rang. She was beginning to lose hope that he would ever call.

"Hello?"

Today she heard the voice she was wishing for. "Hi, Ruby, how are you?" Jason sweetly greeted her.

A big smile spread across her face. "Hi, Jason. It's so good to hear your voice."

"I've been really busy at work. I've had lots of overtime this past week."

They chatted for some time, mostly reviewing details of their conversation aboard ship. He correctly remembered all of the important facts.

"Hey, Ruby, would you like to go to a movie this weekend?"

"I would like that."

"Great. I'll pick you up this Friday at 7:30."

"Perfect."

Their first date was a drive-in movie. She didn't remember the name of the movie or much about the story, because they were too busy kissing and petting. She quickly became aware that his interest in sex was greater than hers. Jason became aroused and tried to force himself on her. She pushed him away; she wasn't ready. They had just met. In fact, she wasn't even aroused like him. She felt so inexperienced. He apologized and promised he could wait.

Ruby was starting to feel some different twinges and tingling in and around her groin. These sensations were new to her, and to her surprise, she was enjoying them. They made her happy. Of course, she only felt these spasms when he was touching her and kissing her body. *This must be love,* she thought.

For their next date, they went to another drive-in movie. He once again constantly pledged his love for her. He told her how much he loved her beautiful slim body, her curves, her full breasts and her hard nipples. Oh, how he enjoyed sucking her nipples. She kind of liked that too and encouraged him to continue. When he touched her between her legs and rubbed his hands up and down the inside of her thighs, she held her breath, because this brought on very new sensations that made her squirm. They were hot twinges that made her feel like her lower body was on fire.

Just before the movie was over, he asked, "Ruby, would you do something really special for me?"

"I guess … what do you want me to do?"

"You could give me amazing pleasure by using your hand. Here, I'll show you," he said taking her hand and gently wrapping it around his very erect cock. "Oh! Wow! That feels wonderful," Jason said as he drew in a gasp of air as if he was having trouble catching his breath when she touched his penis.

She really didn't understand what holding this oversized penis in her hand was going to do for him. This was a very new experience for her. Curiosity and the desire to please him allowed her to step out of her comfort zone and follow his instructions. After all, they were dating like real grown-ups, and she wanted to continue seeing him.

Even though she had never done this before, she hesitantly held on and moved her hand up and down, up and down, caressing him just as she was instructed. She really did want to make him happy, but most of all, she wanted to stop him from pressuring her for sex.

"You're really very sexy. Every time I see you, I want you so much," he said. "I can't wait until I can have you. That's good. Keep going. Don't stop. Ahhh … you make me feel amazing. You are so good at this. Wow!" His body stiffened, he groaned, and then with a big sigh, his body slumped. When he gained his composure, he said, "Thank you so much. I feel like I'm floating on a cloud." His pleasure had come quickly.

Chapter 3
September 1955

Jason lived in Oshawa, a town about forty-five minutes away, but he made the drive to see her frequently over the next three weeks. They spent most of their time together, kissing and petting all evening long. Of course, Jason begged for relief each time. Each time she found this deed less appealing, even though she was becoming quite accomplished at bringing him to a climax with her hands.

She was so naïve. She fell hook, line and sinker for his smooth talk and allowed him to touch parts of her body that had never been touched by a boy before.

By the fifth week, he became even more aggressive and seemed to be less patient with her resistance of his advances. *I wonder if I need to give in to his persistent demands just to keep him interested in me,* she thought. *I really am unsure about this sex thing.*

He told her, "Ruby, I have lots of experience with intercourse. We should go all the way. I promise to be gentle. I'll teach you the wonders of making love. I can make you feel amazingly wonderful. Please believe me; it is the happiest feeling you will ever have.

I've never been in love before, she thought, *so I'm not totally convinced, but I am pretty sure that I'm in love with him. He says he loves me too. What's the harm in exploring? He says that everybody else is doing it. Why not me too?*

Later that week, after some very heated foreplay and the removal of most of their clothing, she had to make a decision. *What is it that I'm waiting for? I want to feel the way he does when I make him come with my hand. I want to know what all the fuss is about. I also want to get rid of the tingling inside me.*

She found herself panting with desire. Her aching crotch felt like it was going to explode. She didn't know what was happening down there or why she felt like this. But she wanted him to ease her discomfort. Jason told her he knew how to make that tingling feeling really amazing. He said he could show her how to get a wonderful climax.

Ruby tried explaining her nervousness and hesitation to Jason. She shyly stated, "But I'm a virgin. I've never been with someone like that ... you know, like, sexually. But when I'm near you, I have these amazing feelings, and I don't know what's going on inside me."

He appealed to her, knowing how vulnerable she was at that moment. "Trust me. I promise, I'll guide you through our first lovemaking experience." He again pressured her: "This will be a very special experience for you. I promise."

She thought, *He's so kind and gentle, and such a gentleman. I have to do it. I want to do it.*

Ruby was more excited and horny than she ever thought a person could be. Truthfully, she knew nothing about being horny. One thing she did know for sure—she wanted relief. Squirming with anticipation and that nagging twitch that needed to be satisfied, she agreed.

He was tender and careful. He cautioned her, "You're a virgin, so your hymen is still intact. I will need to thrust my penis with a little more force than usual just to push through and into your vagina." He presented himself as sort of an expert by using technical jargon.

He did push hard. She tried desperately not to react to the sharp pain. She did all the appropriate moaning and groaning, but then there was nothing. *I guess I didn't know what I was doing. The tingling hasn't completely gone, but I feel better with his post-climax hugging and kissing. Maybe next time!*

Driving back home, Ruby volunteered, "It did hurt, but for only a moment." She added, "You forgot to mention the blood. I think I spoiled my skirt." This gave Ruby a little concern.

Chapter 4
Fall 1955

The rest of that fall, they made love several times on the back seat of his Studebaker, on their local sandy beach, in a wooded area just off the trail, in her bedroom with her family downstairs, and anywhere else they could. Even though she enjoyed his gratification, the desired feeling of satisfaction was not there for her. Even so, they were the horniest couple that couldn't keep their hands off each other for the next three months.

Ruby, in an attempt to educate herself about her part in lovemaking, bought and read every magazine that had an article about sex. These were not exactly teaching tools, as they never really explained to her how to get satisfaction when having sex with the man she loved. This was what she really wanted to know.

Late in the fall, Ruby started to notice changes in her body. It didn't help that she had the flu. She was throwing up every morning lately. Her breasts were getting larger. Jason liked her larger, more sensuous breasts. He couldn't keep his hands off them. He brushed too close by when he passed her or handed her something. He was addicted to her body. Ruby felt more sensual and desired. She was unaware that the change was actually her hormones raging.

She checked her personal calendar and realized that her periods had stopped a few weeks ago. She assumed this might be what happens when you have the flu. But the flu symptoms didn't go away.

Wait, what's going on here? Oh my God. Am I pregnant? The very idea of pregnancy jolted her. *I'm confused. What if I'm really going to have a baby? That can't be. I'm only 16.*

She checked medical encyclopaedias, books, magazines and any other sources that mentioned the word *pregnancy*. She had lots of questions, but she was more desperate than ever for answers.

She wanted to get rid of the flu with Christmas only a week away. They were a large family—five brothers and two sisters, plus spouses and numerous nieces and nephews. Christmas was a huge event when everyone congregated at her parents' house. Gifts were exchanged first, and then an enormous turkey dinner with all of the fixings was devoured.

She didn't tell her mother about her flu or the *other* concern. If she didn't think about it, maybe it would just go away.

Chapter 5
Ruby at Age 11

Ruby remembered times when she had witnessed her mom's bitterness toward members of the family—many times. She didn't understand what was behind her mom's negativity. It might have helped if she did, but Sarah didn't share her feelings. Maybe she just didn't know how.

Ruby's mother was short at five foot nothing. She was very overweight, with several serious ailments. She needed to inject herself with insulin twice each day. Her bad health was not conducive to developing and nurturing healthy relationships with her children or friends.

Ruby thought about other members of her dysfunctional family. Don, her father, considered himself to be a ladies' man. He frequently had affairs with younger women—some as young as her 15 years older sister, Martha. The whole family knew of his preference for younger females. Even now that he was over sixty, his facial skin was smooth and wrinkle-free due to the steam-powered presses he used every day on clothing. He boasted it was like working in a steam bath. He seemed shorter than his stated height of 5 foot 2 inches, as he now had a thick waist with a small pot belly. His sky-blue eyes, one of his most attractive features, were still clear. Of the seven siblings, only two in Ruby's family had the physical appearance of Don—fair hair, wide hips and blue eyes. Ruby was one.

Ruby understood her mother's absolute and complete hatred of men—especially Don, her unfaithful husband. His behaviour had tainted Sarah, and she became very bitter. Family members knew there was no love or kindness coming from Sarah. She had been hurt too deeply. Ruby wondered if this was why she was not a forgiving woman.

Ruby remembered an important time in her past that made her realize her mother would not be there for her now. On Ruby's eleventh birthday, she discovered blood in her panties during a weekend family outing to the local fairgrounds. She was shocked and afraid something awful was happening to her. She was bleeding from somewhere between her legs—from where, she didn't know. It continued all weekend. She remembered thinking, *What's going on? Why am I bleeding?*

Monday morning, she went to school with a wad of tissue stuffed into the crotch of her panties. *I hope I don't bleed onto my clothes during class.* She wore a dark skirt just in case and frequently visited the washroom to change the padding, as there was more blood than Ruby had ever seen before. She knew her mom would be angry if she ruined her skirt.

When Ruby arrived home after school that Monday, her mother was out. Her older married sister Martha met her at the second-floor landing. Martha was living at home temporarily, with her husband and two daughters, as they waited for their newly built house to be ready. Martha was fifteen years older than Ruby. She looked like many of the other family members with her hazel eyes and dark brown—almost black—very short hair and olive skin. It was amazing how much she looked like their mother. Her husband, Charlie, was fun, always joking around. His humour often pulled Martha out of her depressive moods.

Martha handed Ruby a box of sanitary napkins and said, "Here. Use these for the bleeding, and don't let any boy touch you down there."

"How did you know?" Ruby asked.

"Ma saw your underwear when she washed your clothes this morning. So she asked me to give these to you," Martha said, again pointing to the box of napkins.

"But why am I bleeding?" Ruby asked.

"Oh, don't worry. It's okay. Your body is maturing now. Everything will be fine." Martha did her best to reassure Ruby.

Ruby questioned in her mind, *Is this the sex talk my friends say they had with their mothers?* Ruby wondered if her mother didn't know how to broach the subject of menstruation, never mind sex and pregnancy. Maybe it wasn't Ruby she was really mad at after all. Maybe she was mad at herself for not telling Ruby anything about intercourse or the dangers and the consequences of having unprotected sex.

Sarah had grown up in a very strict English home in the early 1900s. She and her family immigrated to Canada from Wales when Sarah was just

6 years old. Her mother, Ruby's grandmother, died during Sarah's very early teenage years.

Ruby thought, *It's funny how the events of one's life are like a chain reaction. We teach our children what we are taught.* Ruby secretly hoped she would be able to break the mould.

Still rehashing the events of years gone by, Ruby remembered a particular event that had a major impact on her young mind. She was 12 years old when she learned her father was a pedophile. This was not something she set out to learn, but she was volunteered by her mother and older sister to be "the watcher." Her responsibilities consisted of watching out for the young girls around the house—Ruby's friends or any other young female visitors. Specifically, when the girls were in her father's company, Ruby was assigned the task of letting one of the older female family members—like her mother, sister, or sisters-in-law—know that so-and-so was sitting on Dad's lap. Ruby hated that role as much as she hated her father at that point. One thing Ruby knew for sure was that her children would never be left alone with their grandfather.

Another month and still no period, she made an appointment with the doctor. He had been their family physician for as far back as she could remember. The doctor's receptionist responded to Ruby's request for an appointment: "Will 10:00 a.m. next Tuesday work for you?"

"Yes, thank you."

Chapter 6

Unwanted News

With a severe case of nerves, Ruby arrived at the doctor's office. She concentrated on putting one foot in front of the other, fearing she might stumble. Hesitantly, she ambled into the reception area and approached the wicket. In a subdued voice, she said to the young lady wearing a white uniform, "Ruby Dalton for my ten o'clock appointment."

Ruby was relieved when the receptionist invited her to have a seat. She wasn't sure she could stand on her wobbly legs much longer.

The whole time she waited, her heart was pounding. Dreading the receptionist's voice, she finally heard, "Miss Dalton, the doctor will see you now."

Walking hesitantly, she made her way down the hall to the cold sterile examination room. Nurse Jane walked alongside and attempted to draw more information from Ruby. "Can you tell me why you're here to see the doctor?"

Ruby seemed to be inspecting the floor. Afraid to make eye contact, she kept her eyes focused down. In a faint voice, she said, "I think I have the flu. I've been throwing up a lot lately."

"How are your periods?" Nurse Jane asked.

Ruby immediately feared the nurse suspected something other than the flu. *How did she know?*

"I haven't had a period for more than a month," Ruby quietly shared, as if it were a secret.

Nurse Jane led her to the examination table. "Please remove everything from the waist down. Get up on this table and put the sheet over you. The doctor will be in shortly."

Lying very still on the thin paper that covered the elevated table, Ruby tried not to move because the crinkling sounded like glass breaking. All alone in the examination room, which had a slightly antiseptic odour, Ruby nervously waited for what seemed like an eternity. Her thoughts were running rampant. *If I'm pregnant, what will Doctor Martin think of me? Will he think I'm a bad person? I'm so scared. What am I going to do?* Her stomach growled.

She was quickly brought back to reality when the doctor entered the room and said, "Hello, Ruby. I haven't seen you for quite some time. How's your mother?" Doctor Martin could see how frightened Ruby was and tried to ease the tension.

"Mom's okay. She still gets those bad headaches." Ruby was willing to play the game and put off the inevitable diagnosis.

"That's too bad. I believe she has an appointment later this week. But you came to see me. Tell me why you're here?" he asked in his most personable reassuring voice.

"I think I have the flu," she said, sticking to the diagnosis that would please her most.

"Nurse Jane tells me that you missed your last period. Is that right?"

"Yes," she said. Lowering her gaze, she responded in an almost inaudible voice, "Probably because of the flu. I've been throwing up a lot." Then she shivered more from the thought of pregnancy than the coolness of the sterile room.

Putting on stretchy vinyl gloves now covered with a clear gooey substance, he said, "Okay, let me examine you, and maybe we will know more."

The examination was humiliating and a little painful. The doctor looked up at her with a puzzled expression. "Are you sexually active?"

"Yes," she whispered, changing her sight line to the window beyond Doctor Martin. She also wondered if it made a difference if she wasn't enjoying sex.

"Sorry, Ruby, I think you're about three months pregnant. I took a uterine swab, but I'm pretty sure my first diagnosis is correct. I'll send this sample to the lab to be tested."

She knew before he finished his first sentence that she did not have the flu. *Thank goodness I'm lying down, or I'd likely faint.*

The doctor's voice bounced around in her head and echoed through the examination room. He had just confirmed her worst nightmare. She was in a daze. *This cannot be happening to me.*

"Ruby, we need to have a chat now, or you can make another appointment.

You're looking a little pale; maybe you should have a seat in the waiting room for a few minutes. I'd like you to come back to see me when the news sinks in, and you've had a chance to talk to the father and your mother. Being about three months pregnant, there are things you need to do, like eating healthy and taking special vitamins with iron. If the vomiting continues, we can give you something for that."

"When will the baby be born?" she asked, more from curiosity than needing to know for planning.

"Your baby will likely be born around the beginning of July. That's a rough guesstimate, of course." Doctor Martin put a comforting hand on her shoulder.

She knew he saw the fear in her eyes. As he left the room, he quietly asked Nurse Jane, "I wonder if our very young mother-to-be has a decent support system. Would you mind asking?"

"Of course, doctor. I'll give Ruby some pamphlets with phone numbers for some resources." Nurse Jane turned to Ruby and said, "When you finish dressing, you can pick up an envelope at reception with some information on places that will help you."

Mechanically, Ruby tried to get dressed. She fumbled nervously with her underwear, her hands trembling. Two tries later, She finally got a foot into the leg of her jeans. Several attempts later, she gave up on the waist button and zipper. She pulled down her sweater to cover the gaping open space. *Oh, hell, I'm wearing my long winter jacket. It'll be covered.* Her waist had expanded from the pregnancy, she knew now, and not from overeating during the holidays.

On her way out, she stopped to speak with the older receptionist and get the envelope with her name on it. "Tell Doctor Martin I'll call and make another appointment. Bye." Navigating more by habit than intention, Ruby made her way out of the doctor's office, along the narrow institutional green hallway and down the stairs. She was in a fog. She sat bolt upright on the bus and stared out the window. She barely remembered the trip home.

How could this happen? I think Jason is not as well-versed about sex or pregnancy as he thought he was. I also realize that I know even less. From what I've been reading, he really should have worn a condom.

Having a baby on TV shows looked extremely painful. *What have I done? The women scream at the top of their lungs and cry. Now that scares the hell out of me.*

Ruby stopped at her local convenience store before walking home.

Clutching the envelope, she was desperate to find magazines or books—which she preferred—that could help her understand the changes that were happening to her body.

I have fretted for too long. I must somehow get the courage to call Jason and tell him the news. This is likely the last conversation I'll ever have with him. He'll probably leave me to fend for myself. Abandon me—after all, it is me that's going to have a baby, not him.

After several tentative attempts, Ruby finally gathered the courage to dial Jason's number.

"Hello?"

The sound of his voice gave her nerve to continue. "Hi, Jason. How are you?"

"I'm good. We're very busy at work right now. I'm not complaining, because I earn lots more money."

Ruby tried to be patient and let him tell her about work, but she knew her announcement was way more important than anything he had to say. She blurted out, "I went to see my doctor today."

"Are you not feeling well?"

"I'm pregnant."

"*Really.* Are you sure?"

"Yes. My doctor, unfortunately, confirmed that I'm about three months pregnant. I'm really scared," she whispered into the receiver. Sarah was in the next room, watching her daily soaps.

"Oh my God. Have you told your mother yet?"

She avoided the question. "I feel funny all of the time, and the constant vomiting leaves a really bad taste in my mouth." She pulled a face just like when she smelled or ate something yucky.

"I'm sorry you're not feeling well. Did you tell your mother yet?"

"No. I'm actually dreading telling her. I think she'll be really angry," Ruby shared in a very low voice, now fighting back tears.

He heard the crack in her voice. "Ruby, please don't cry. It'll be all right. I promise. But you have to tell her. I'll tell my parents tonight," he said as if he was accepting some responsibility for her pregnancy.

"Jason, what do I do now?" Ruby asked when she realized he wasn't going to abandon her. His acceptance allowed her to gather a little courage.

"I'm Catholic. We don't believe in abortion, so that's not an option," he firmly stated.

"Abortion? What's that?" she questioned, and then she continued before he could respond, "Is that something I should consider? I don't know anything about abortion."

"No, sweetie, nothing for you to worry about. Please, just tell your mother."

She knew he regretted bringing up the subject of abortion. She heard the hesitation in his voice. This wouldn't be his plan. She did wonder why he brushed off her comments and questions. Ruby was sure he didn't know the answer to her questions anyway.

She stood silently holding the receiver. Her feet were frozen to the spot. *What should I do? Oh, I feel sick to my stomach, but this time it definitely isn't morning sickness. I'm so afraid.* She clutched her tummy as a wave of nausea came over her. She managed to muster the courage to agree. In an almost incoherent voice, she mumbled, "Okay … you're right. I need to tell her. I don't mind telling you, I'm really, really scared. I wish you were here for moral support."

He emphatically stated, "Sorry, Ruby, but your mother scares the hell out of me. Every time I'm with you, she gives me that look like she hates me. She'll dislike me even more now. I can't handle that—at least not right now."

Ruby believed that deep down Jason did want to help her, but she knew he had developed a serious fear of her mother. When she thought about her mother and how she gave Jason her nasty looks and stares, she understood his dread. Ruby hadn't thought about her mother becoming Jason's mother-in-law. She wondered if her mother would ever welcome Jason into the family. The whole mess caused a cold shudder to rush over her whole body.

Bringing herself back to the conversation, Ruby offered, "I don't know how she's going to react. I wish this was someone else's life, not mine."

"Please, I don't want to hear you say that. We'll be okay. Just tell your mother. Call me later tonight or tomorrow after I get home from work. Whatever happens, I want to know. Good luck, Ruby. I'll be thinking about you."

Speaking softly, with her left hand cupped over the receiver, she said, "Okay. I'll probably talk to you tomorrow."

In a deep trance of reflection, she stared blankly into space. Ruby placed the receiver onto the phone cradle. With reluctance, she walked slowly—oh so very slowly—into the living room. *I wonder if I need to first practice what I'm going to say. I know how she overreacts to the least little thing. This is no small issue. She'll blow up and start putting me down like my feelings don't count. How do I tell her? Will she care that this talk is really important to me? I wonder how she'll accept my news. She may toss me out onto the street. Then what would I do?*

Entering the living room, she looked at her mother engrossed in *The Guiding Light*. Sarah never missed an episode. *Maybe this is not a good time. We're never permitted to bother her when she's watching her soaps. I'll come back later.* Ruby moved as if to walk away, sidestepping the conversation. *Who am I kidding?* she scolded herself. *Avoiding telling her will solve nothing. Putting this off isn't an option. I must have this conversation.*

She made several false starts, but eventually she got the courage to confess. She timidly said, "Mom ... I ... Mom, I saw Doctor Martin today."

With eyes straight ahead, still watching the TV, her mother said, "Why?"

Ruby drew in a long deep breath and squeezed her eyes almost closed, dreading her next sentence. She hesitated, and then she gathered a little bit of courage. Taking a deep breath and then exhaling very slowly, she put off uttering the worst news ever. Sheepishly, she lowered her eyes, focused on the floor and said, "I thought I had the flu."

"Okay," Sarah said, half listening but still visibly glued to her TV.

Ruby wasn't unhappy that her mother's attention was still on her soaps. She paused, took another deep breath and then quickly blurted out, "He said that I'm pregnant." Then she slumped into a chair out of relief from finally revealing her secret.

Her mother slowly turned her head away from the television. Now glaring at Ruby with pursed lips, she scowled and then said in a scolding, angry tone, "You're a stupid girl, Ruby. Do you even know who the father is?"

"Yes. It's Jason." That was all she managed to say. *She thinks I'm a slut and sleeping around.* She started to cry.

"I thought you were raised better than to be sleeping with every boy who looks in your direction. Have you no self-respect?" her mother hissed at her.

Mustering more courage between tears and sobbing, she raised her voice, speaking over her mother's barrage of insults. "It's not like that. We're in love." She attempted to convey more positive details, but her mother raised her voice and yelled louder than Ruby.

"Well, you can just kiss your entire life, hopes and dreams goodbye. You're probably going to be on welfare at the rate you're going."

"Please, Mom, try to understand. I ..."

"I *do* understand you have ruined your life, young lady. What about school?"

"I guess I'll have to quit." This realization had a bigger impact on Ruby than she ever thought. She hadn't considered this obvious consequence. She loved school.

"What about your job?"

"They let me work part-time …"

"Without money, you can't buy food and pay for rent."

"I'm trying to tell you, they hired me part-time when school resumed in September. Maybe they'll let me work full-time now."

Ruby was getting frustrated with Sarah interrupting her each time she tried to speak. Her mom was not interested in listening to anything Ruby had to say.

"Mom, we're in love."

"Love?" her mother spat. "What do you know about love? I'll tell you right now, you'll either marry that guy or I'll send you to a home for bad girls to have the baby. Then we'll put it up for adoption. I don't want any more babies around here. I'm done with shitty diapers."

Ruby cried and blurted out, "It's not like that. We want to be a family." She had lost the battle of fighting back the tears that were waiting to flood down her face. Ruby tried very hard to control her emotions, but her hormones caused mood swings like she'd never experienced.

"Don't you know that once these types of guys get into your pants, they don't want you around anymore? I thought you were smarter. You turn out to be the dumbest of them all." Her mother ranted on and on for what felt like hours.

Ruby couldn't take it anymore. Being beaten up mentally by her own mother was hurtful. Ruby felt a total lack of support or compassion from Sarah. She ran up the two flights of stairs to her bedroom crying and shouting back at her angry mother, "It would've been nice if you offered me some support. The last thing I needed was to be verbally battered by you."

She ran as fast as her young legs could carry her to her place of solitude. The place where she always found solace was her bedroom in the attic of their three-story house.

Normally Ruby would carefully remove the decorative hot pink pillows and the matching comforter with bunches of white roses growing all over it. Not today. She was blinded to her surroundings by the flood of tears that poured from her now-red-rimmed eyes. She slammed the door shut and flopped on top of her bed. *Why does she always put me down? She makes me feel alone and unwanted. I could use some kindness right now. My whole world has* come crashing down around me, and instead of comfort, she just puts me down more. What's going to happen to me? She cried and cried until sleep rescued her from her misery.

Next morning, she lay in her bed half awake and remembered last evening's angry response to her announcement. Feeling beaten and vulnerable, she snuggled under her warm cozy comforter. She purposely pulled the bedding even closer for both the physical and the emotional comfort she needed. Glancing at the windows, she saw that Jack Frost had been busy while she slept. She liked to imagine that the frosty markings on her windows represented artistic masters. Sometimes she visualized trees; other times, whole scenes with water and mountains and even flowers created by nature's painter, Jack Frost.

The morning sun now peeked through the frosty windows, and the brightness brought her back to reality. She was pregnant, had raging hormones and was filled with fear of the unknown. She once again let the tears that had pooled in her eyes overflow and run out and down her temples, wetting her pretty pink pillowcase.

Ruby understood that her mom had issues, but that was not a good-enough excuse for Sarah's hurtful behaviour the night before. Ruby had feelings too. Recalling the cause of last evening's scolding, her hands moved to her tummy. A little bulge had already formed. *One thing I know for sure—I will be a better mother.*

Chapter 7

A Not So Merry Christmas

Several days before Christmas, Ruby telephoned Jason again to report on the conversation she'd had with her mother. "Hi, Jason. How are you?" She was unsure about how to start the discussion or what to say.

"I'm good. Are you okay?"

"Yeah, I'm okay."

"How did it go with your mother?" he asked, showing genuine concern.

"No different than I thought it would be. She yelled and called me terrible names until I couldn't take it any longer. I went to bed and cried myself to sleep."

"Hey, I'm sorry your mom treated you that way. I really like you. We can get married if you want. My parents are okay with the prospect of a new daughter-in-law, because they're quite fond of you already. My mother's also pleased that we're giving her a grandchild. You know these Italian mothers. They love children and big families."

She wanted to scream, *But I'm only 16! I have my whole life ahead of me. I had plans.* Ruby's mind was racing around in all directions. *Married! This definitely does not fit into my plans.*

"Jason," she said, "I'm confused about everything that's happening right now. I wanted to go back to school. Did I ever tell you that I've always wanted to be a nurse?"

"No."

"I feel like I'm going through a lot these days."

"Does this mean you don't want to marry me or have our baby?"

"It's more than that. It's like I'm losing myself."

"Ruby, you're okay. You'll be fine. Please believe me."

"I know. Let's talk more later when all these feelings settle."

She couldn't, nor did she want to, imagine what it would be like for her baby to be raised in a foster home. What if some really mean people adopted her child? What if the man was a pedophile? She'd rather live on welfare than not know her baby and its future. When she weighed her options, she had to agree that marriage might be better than a home for bad girls and adoption of her baby. She decided that her plans would just have to wait.

Chapter 8

Sharing Family Secrets

A few days later, Ruby and Debbie—dressed in their winter jackets, scarves, mitts and toques—met on Ruby's front porch. One of their favourite places was the big old brown plush comfy sofa chair there. They wrapped themselves up in a blanket to protect them from the freezing cold, just as they had done so many times in the past. Then Ruby confided in her friend Debbie, "I told my mother about being pregnant. She was not happy. She yelled at me and called me horrible names. I went to bed just to get away from her."

"Don't worry," said Debbie. "I think this is all so exciting. We can have a wedding shower for you and then a baby shower. I'm going to start planning right now. I'm so jealous." Debbie, true to her romantic personality, was eager to do all the things she had witnessed in movies, TV and magazines.

"Deb, you know, I've mentioned to you before about being 'the watcher,' right?"

"Yeah. Your dad always seemed so nice."

"I've always wanted to tell you the rest of the story," Ruby said, as it was apparent that she was in a confessing mood. "I was passed over for his sexual interference, because his prey became the younger girls. I was too old for him. I looked it up in the dictionary. It said that he was in the category of being a preferential abuser. That means he was exclusively sexually attracted to children who had not begun puberty. You know, those who haven't started their periods. Thank goodness I was spared."

Debbie said, "I've never met a pedophile before; just knowing your dad

Ruby Monroe

is one is really creepy. He's never approached me, you know. I would never let him touch me," Debbie quickly added, just to keep the record straight.

"Deb, you're too old for him." They both had a good laugh that, at 16, they would be too old for anything.

"You know," Ruby added, "it doesn't help matters that my mother's in denial. To my knowledge, she hasn't ever confronted him. When I get married, someone else will need to take over as the watcher." Ruby wanted to change to a different subject. Talking about her father made her angry. She found the subject even more depressing than being pregnant at 16.

Later that week, on a very cold snowy day, Ruby and Debbie once again dressed for the frigid January temperature and snuggled up in their favourite cozy chair on the gray-painted wooden front porch of Ruby's three-story house. Ruby confided, "Deb, the family was so happy when Mom finally kicked my dad out the day after Christmas. When he came home from work, he found all of his clothes and belongings in boxes on the front porch."

Chapter 9

1956 Brings New Beginnings

The happy three-months-pregnant couple got married on Friday, January 13, at city hall. Jason and his best man, Eddy, wore similar outfits: black slacks and open-neck white dress shirts. Debbie in her new mint-green frock happily served as maid of honour. Ruby wore a fairly plain knee-length periwinkle blue dress with a slightly gathered skirt to hide the bump that seemed to grow larger daily. She carried a small bouquet of daisies held together with a white ribbon tied in a bow.

They blushed as they nervously repeated their vows. The rings that Jason had bought were exchanged. The Justice of the Peace proclaimed, without prejudice toward this very young expectant couple, "You are now husband and wife." He looked at the spectators and the other couples waiting to tie the knot and said, "Let me introduce you to Jason and Ruby Monroe." Then he looked directly at Jason and said, "You may now kiss the bride."

Ruby liked the sound of that. They kissed and hugged. Ruby beamed with pleasure. She was so very happy.

Ruby's now very pregnant older sister Martha invited family and close friends to a reception to celebrate Jason and Ruby's marriage. The festivities took place downstairs in the recreation room, which was decorated with streamers and balloons. Many practical gifts were presented to the newlyweds, who were in need of absolutely everything to set up their first home and start their new life together.

Music flooded the basement recreation room and flowed out of the open doors and windows, meeting the January chill. Charlie, Martha's husband, was somewhat of a chef. Actually, he had been a cook for the army when he served in Germany. He still knew how to prepare good food for a crowd. Everyone liked Charlie—especially his broad smile and the fact that he was always ready with a joke or a wisecrack. He wasn't intimidating to anyone at 5 feet 7 inches and 180 pounds. His daughters admitted to loving their dad and his antics. He was always ready with hugs and kisses for them.

The partygoers enjoyed the fare and drinks. The dancing continued into the early morning. Ruby and Jason happily accepted everyone's best wishes and celebrated with the guests until the last person left.

There was very little spare money, so they spent their wedding night in her third-floor attic bedroom. They were happy and exhausted.

Jason gently kissed Ruby and then smiled a very mischievous, knowing grin. Caressing her growing bump and then her enlarged breasts, he whispered in her ear, "Let's make love and consummate our new status as Mr. and Mrs. Jason Monroe."

"Sounds like a plan to me," Ruby agreed. "I thought you would never ask."

"I love you so much, Ruby. I can't ever remember feeling like this about anyone ever before," he said as he pulled the covers back so he could gaze at her voluptuous pregnant body.

Neither one wanted foreplay. Both were so horny after all of the day's excitement, plus the dancing and cuddling at their party.

"Babe, you've got the best body," said Jason. "I want to make love to you over and over again. Sometimes when I'm driving home after seeing you, I ejaculate. I can't help it. I'm addicted to you." He was getting ready to come. She could always tell because he made so much noise. She wondered if the noises, groaning and talking dirty was for him or if he was trying to make her horny too. If so, he wasn't succeeding.

Chapter 10

New Adventure: March 1956

Ruby and Jason checked the classified ads every day for flats they could afford. There were several small affordable accommodations they visited, but these were either no bigger than a closet or a cockroach haven. Every day they were more disappointed, and they started to think they would need to stay longer in Ruby's bedroom up in the attic.

Ruby felt their marriage couldn't survive too much longer in their current environment. There was very little privacy, because Rob, her innocent slightly older brother, had the bedroom right across the hall from their room. Ruby's mom and sweet Marianne, her youngest sister, both slept in their bedrooms on the floor below.

"Jason, I'm beginning to think we'll be here for our whole married life."

"Have faith, baby. We have time. No one wants us to have our own place more than me."

Just when they were about to give up the hunt, totally frustrated, they found a cute cozy fully furnished second-floor rental in a well-kept older house located in the Upper Beach area. It was in a great hippie neighbourhood not far from the lake—a three-minute walk to public transportation and about a fifteen-minute walk to her family home. Most importantly, the price was right. It was perfect.

Their new apartment was, in reality, just a very large bright sunny room with a small bay window facing the busy street below. The single room was set up to accommodate cooking, eating, and TV-watching or visiting. There was a windowless smaller room with a lumpy mattress on a double bed that took up almost the whole space. There was an unrelated dresser with chipped paint and one very small closet. They shared the compact bathroom with the couple from the third floor.

But who cared? They were in love, married and having a baby. Life was wonderful—a fairy tale for sure. Ruby was all grown up now, an adult. Soon she'd be a mother.

Jason searched the job ads and attended several interviews the first week they were at their new abode. "Jason, what are we going to do if you can't find a job?" asked Ruby. "I won't be able to work at the telephone company too much longer, being pregnant and all."

A few days later, he rushed home and boasted, "I have a job at the largest public utility company around here, Shore Gas. You know how much I like working with numbers. Well, I'm going to be a junior clerk in their accounting department. To think that I was apprenticing to be an electrician! This job is so much better. I'm so excited. I would never have dreamed I would qualify." He was grinning from ear to ear and bursting with pride.

"That's wonderful!" said Ruby. "Congratulations, Jason. See, everything is going to work out for us. I'm so happy."

"Best of all," he added, "I will make enough money to pay all of our expenses, even when you go on maternity leave." He radiated happiness. There was a positive change in his mood and a bounce in his step.

Fortunately, back when she had realized she was pregnant, Ruby had been able to get re-employed at the telephone company as an operator. She had worked there the previous summer, so they were happy to take her back. She was already trained for the position. Life was perfect: they had good jobs, a place to live and a baby on the way. They hugged, kissed and celebrated by making love several times.

Now they were really hungry. Jason, protected from the blustery cold weather in his fur-trimmed hooded winter coat, hat and gloves, ran to the pizza joint around the corner on Queen Street and ordered their favourite pepperoni and cheese pizza. He knew by now that Ruby didn't have much experience cooking.

Martha, Ruby's older sister, was pregnant and expecting in March, a month away. She telephoned Ruby and proposed, "Our second-floor flat is available. Would you and Jason like to rent it? The flat is furnished; all you will need are linens, bedding and towels. We'll help you with those items until you guys can buy your own. We want to make sure the rent is very affordable for you."

Ruby knew that Martha was worried about her little sister going through her pregnancy all alone at such a young age. Ruby had been told by friends and relatives that they were concerned about the two of them, as she and Jason had no experience with married life, never mind caring for a baby.

Jason and Ruby talked the proposal over for all of five minutes. Ruby immediately called Martha back and said, "We would love to accept your generous offer, Martha. We also have good news. Jason got a good job, and he's starting tomorrow."

Ruby could hear the smile in Martha's voice as she said, "That is good to hear. I think my little sister is going to be just fine."

Jason and Ruby had been renting on a monthly basis, so they gave their notice and moved at the end of the month.

Jason was excited because he really liked Martha's husband, Charlie. They joked and laughed at each other's silly jokes and antics. Their relationship flourished.

The newlyweds spent most of their time on the first level of the house with Martha, Charlie, and their two daughters, plus Martha's newly arrived infant, Julie. It was fun for everyone. Due to their age difference, Martha and Ruby had developed somewhat of a mother-daughter relationship, though not entirely.

Charlie and Jason frequently sat on the front porch in their favourite rocking chairs drinking beer from bottles and discussing the world at large, their favourite sports teams and the passing traffic on their busy street.

Ruby wanted to learn to cook. She practiced on Jason and her sister's family. Martha belonged to a food club that sold frozen foods. The order was delivered every two weeks directly to the house. Ruby learned that Martha's idea of cooking was opening a bag of frozen vegetables, frozen French fries and some sort of meat—frozen, of course. Martha heated everything in the oven on cookie sheets just before putting it on plates and then placing the plates on the table. The food was dry and unappetizing.

Jason joked, "Now I know why they use so much ketchup."

Ruby knew that Jason, with his Italian upbringing, did not appreciate this bland processed frozen food. Ruby was encouraged to cook more creatively.

Jason suggested, "Ruby, I think you should take some cooking classes. This way you can learn to prepare more appetizing food, just like my mom cooks."

"I agree, and I will sign up for cooking classes after the baby is born. I'm sure I'll have more time once this large lump on my belly becomes a real baby."

Money was tight for both families, so they spent much of their socializing time playing board games and cards. These were some of the best days in Ruby's memory of her younger years.

One day, Martha asked Ruby, "Would you like to learn how to bathe a baby?"

"Yes," Ruby replied. "I would really like that."

"Watch me. I'll show you how, and then you can wash Julie and I'll supervise." Ruby also gave the infant her bottle for practice.

Now with her much larger belly lump, she was delighted and scared, because the birth seemed more real. Ruby shared, "Martha, I can't wait until my baby is born. I am going to love being a mom so much. I know I'll be a good mother."

This was also her promise to her unborn baby as she rubbed her belly in response to the movement that felt like butterflies fluttering around within her tummy.

Everything was working out just fine. Ruby and Jason went out for walks each night; they held hands and talked about the events and people in their day. This was Ruby's prenatal exercise and their special time together.

It was at about this time that there appeared to be a tiny crack in their perfect union. The closer she got to the scheduled delivery date, the less interest she had in sex. Her once slim body now had an ever-growing bulge. She waddled like a duck. She felt fat, awkward and unattractive. It became very difficult to tie her shoelaces, pull on slacks, or do anything that required her to bend over. In fact, her feet seemed to have disappeared.

During her next appointment with her doctor, she broached the subject of having sex so near to her delivery date.

He suggested, "Ruby your lack of interest in sex is just hormones. You have nothing at all to worry about. Everything will go back to normal once the baby's born. Aside from how awkward you are feeling, you could avoid getting an infection and possible premature birth if you refrained from sexual penetration during this last trimester."

Ruby was okay with the doctor's suggestion because she was concerned that intercourse could hurt the baby. Jason, however, did not appreciate being cut off from sex—not one little bit. He would go for hours and sometimes days without speaking to Ruby. She had a difficult enough time dealing with her own wacky hormones and mood swings. She just didn't know how to explain to Jason how she was feeling with her physical and mental changes. His tantrums were complicating an already difficult time for her.

It was during one of these withdrawn moods of his that he lashed out at her and slapped her right across her face. She was shocked, hurt and surprised. Ruby cried like a baby, and through sobs, she managed to ask, "Why did you do that?"

She didn't know it at the time, but that step over the line by Jason was a major breaking point in their relationship. She had no idea that things were about to get worse—a lot worse.

Of course, he apologized profusely, declared his love and promised he would never hit her again. It was a promise she would hear many more times. She learned quite soon that his apologies were like a soap bubble: shivering and empty.

Chapter 11

Arrival of a Bundle of Joy

It was a beautiful, sunny July morning. A happy day. Ruby was looking forward to sitting outside and maybe having a BBQ with Jason and her sister's family.

She woke up very early with the strongest urge to urinate. Still half asleep, she walked into the bathroom. To her surprise, she felt a very thick fluid run down the inside of her thighs. In the bathroom, she investigated. There was washed-out red-coloured fluid mixed into the clearer thick liquid. She remembered this was a topic discussed at her prenatal classes and came to the conclusion that it might be time to go to the hospital.

Now wide awake, she felt the frequent cramps in her lower pelvic area. Martha had done a good job of explaining to Ruby what would happen and when it was time to go to the hospital. Ruby put on a sanitary napkin to avoid making a mess of Martha's hardwood floors and then hurried back to their bedroom. Shaking Jason, she announced, "Jason, get up … Jason, please wake up. I think we need to go to the hospital. I'm pretty sure my water just broke. Our baby is coming!"

"What did you say?"

"Get dressed! We are going to be parents today."

Jason jumped out of bed, dressed and then rushed around frantically and erratically. He was totally disorganized. Fortunately, at Martha's insistence, Ruby had packed a hospital bag. She was ready.

Ruby knocked on Martha and Charlie's bedroom door and told them that she and Jason were on their way to the hospital. She apologized for the mess on the bathroom floor. Ruby said she was afraid to bend down to clean it up because she was in labour and the pains were already four minutes apart.

Martha whispered, "I'll clean it up. Just get to the hospital. I don't want you giving birth in the car."

"Thanks, Martha. I'm scared. Is that normal?"

"Yes. Now get going. We'll talk later." Martha tried to minimize details about giving birth. After three children, she was all too familiar with the process.

They drove the short distance to the hospital, and the attendant took Ruby in a wheelchair to the labour area on the third floor. Fearfully, Ruby settled in for the birthing process. Ruby at 16 was very timid and frightened by the screaming coming from some of the cubicles. It sounded like the women were being tortured. She asked the nurse, "Why are those ladies in such pain? Will my pains be that bad?"

"No. Everyone reacts to pain differently. You're doing fine. Don't worry, sweetie," said Bev, the birthing nurse assigned to her.

She asked another nurse, "Are they dying? They're really scaring me."

Sharon, a tall, efficient and caring nurse, said, "You don't need to worry. Your body's young, and it's much easier for a younger person because your bones are more pliable. Believe me, it really is easier for someone with a young body to give birth." It was true. Ruby never screamed once. She suffered through her pain in silence.

She was administered anaesthetic when it was time to deliver. Thank goodness she was really groggy through the actual birth. Ruby was happy that the labour pains were gone and replaced by a crying baby.

"Ruby, congratulations!" Doctor Martin announced with the enthusiasm of a young intern. "You have a beautiful, healthy and very loud baby boy—six pounds and five ounces. He's perfect: ten fingers and ten toes."

Jason had gone home to catch up on his sleep. Doctor Martin telephoned him with the good news. Jason was so excited about his new parental status that he ran out of the house in his stocking feet. A neighbour who Jason had announced his new fatherhood status to mentioned that he might want to go back into the house and put on his shoes.

Ruby and Jason chose to name their scrawny, red, wrinkled, wailing baby Matthew John Monroe. It was a name fit for a future executive, statesman or a president. They nicknamed him Matt.

The nurses in the maternity ward had dubbed Ruby the "child mother." She was overwhelmed with her new motherhood. At the tender age of

16, she certainly had a lot to learn. Absolutely everything was new to her. Breastfeeding her new infant was not as easy or natural as she thought it would be. With perseverance, she did master this new skill. Martha had not breastfed any of her babies, so there had been no instructions in advance.

Jason did all the silly things new fathers do, like buying the baby boy toys that he would not be able to use for about three years—well, at least until after he learned to walk. Ruby smiled. *This* was the man she loved.

It was a huge adjustment for them to create a family atmosphere. They had only known each other for eleven months in total. Some people's engagements lasted longer than that. They met, courted, got pregnant, got married and had a baby all in less than one year. Ruby was still 16 years old.

Martha helped Ruby with baby care information. She also offered advice on child-rearing. Martha and Charlie were now veterans, as parents of three girls. When Martha's newest baby grew out of her tiny baby things, they were passed along to Matt. Ruby only accepted baby clothes that were in a neutral color. No pink pyjamas or girly blankets for her special son.

Chapter 12

The Next Phase: June 1957

Ruby's mother loaned the newlyweds money for a down payment so they could purchase a charming little white clapboard bungalow. The floor space wasn't quite 1,000 square feet. It did have a large backyard for 1-year-old Matt to play in. A swing set, a gift from Jason's family, took up about one-quarter of the yard.

Their cute little bungalow was just up the street from Ruby's mother's house. Sarah held the mortgage to their new house; this was what made it possible for them to purchase the house. Neither Ruby nor Jason could qualify as single or combined applicants. They definitely would not have been approved for a mortgage at a bank. As it was, they went into debt to purchase furniture, window coverings and appliances—absolutely everything. Ruby wanted to make it feel like a real home.

Their first family get-together at the new house was for Matt's first birthday party. Jason was in charge of the BBQ. Hamburgers and hot dogs plus a store-bought chocolate iced and balloon-decorated birthday cake made up the menu. Everyone took photos of the beautiful blonde 1-year-old. This was a happy time—maybe one of the best in her memory of that house.

Among the people Ruby invited were her in-laws, Angela and Tom Monroe. She really loved them. They were both kind and caring folks, and they always treated her like their own daughter. She felt closer to her mother-in-law than to her own mother. The in-laws had five grown children—two daughters and three sons.

Jason got his mojo back. They made passionate love more frequently now that they were alone in their own home. Ruby rationalized the change in his behaviour as just needing to be in his own comfortable space with privacy. They partied and visited with friends and relatives. For several years, things were more good than bad.

Ruby was now 18 and interested in learning more about her body and how to satisfy Jason's immense sexual appetite. She wanted to know more about the G-spot or the "big O." She read everything she could find on both subjects.

One day, Ruby read a pocketbook that was very descriptive about the lovemaking of the hero and heroine. Suddenly, it all clicked for her. She needed to do more moving and tilt up her pelvis during sex. She practiced repositioning her pelvis and tilting it upward just like the book described. This permitted her vagina to be in the right position to accept his penis. When Jason inserted his erect penis into her moist vagina in this new position, his penis entered right on the path of the much desired G-spot.

Then, during one hot passionate lovemaking session, she experienced the most wonderful mind-blowing satisfying climax. She smiled in the darkness of their bedroom. Silently she congratulated herself. She knew her search for the big O was over. So this was what all the fuss was about. These feelings gave her the most wonderful sensual satisfaction.

She knew she would really enjoy sex now. Jason would be more attentive for sure. Most importantly, she had finally reached the previously elusive, wonderful orgasm. Ruby was confident that she could experience this amazing sensation each and every time they had sex. She glowed with pleasure and brimmed over with sexuality.

Ruby felt she could conquer the world. Jason was more than pleased with himself. He took credit for her pleasure during their lovemaking. He wanted to make love every single night. One of their favourite times to make love was after they showered on Saturday and Sunday mornings. She never objected. It made him happy, and she was very happy with her newfound gratification during sex. In fact, she was often the one who initiated sex. Who wouldn't?

Ruby boasted to Jason, "I think I'm addicted to sex."

She often joked when they finished making love, "You know, I was just checking to make sure the big O is still there, and I'm pleased to report that it is."

"That's my sexy lady," Jason praised her.

Ruby's younger sister Marianne loved and was totally devoted to her nephew Matt. She was three years younger than Ruby, just 15, and a good-looking girl with dark hair and hazel-coloured eyes. She lived at home with their mother on the same street as Ruby, so she frequently dropped in to see Matt, the apple of her eye. Matt and Marianne would play for hours at a time.

Marianne offered, "I'll babysit Matt anytime—just let me know. The price will be right, *free*, so don't give me any of that crap about not being able to afford a sitter. You guys go out and have fun."

This was very generous of Marianne, but they knew her real motivation: she wanted to be around Matt every waking moment.

They took advantage of Marianne's big-heartedness. Jason and Ruby developed a more active social life thanks to Marianne. Life was wonderful.

One day, Ruby telephoned her sister and asked, "Marianne, would you like to look after Matt this Saturday evening?"

Marianne responded, "I'm sorry, but I'm busy. Maybe I'll be free another time."

This became Marianne's response each and every time Ruby asked. Ruby wondered, *Why the change?*

Several months later, Marianne dropped by one day when she didn't see Jason's white Studebaker parked in its usual spot in front of the house. She knew Ruby would be home alone. She finally gathered the courage to tell her sister, "I don't like saying no to you every time you ask me to look after Matt. It's just that I'm not comfortable around Jason. The last two times he drove me home, he made a pass at me."

"What are you saying? What do you mean?" Ruby questioned.

"He tried to kiss me and feel my breasts. I'm so sorry, Ruby. I really miss Matt. In fact, sometimes I drop by during the day when I see him out front playing. I still enjoy visiting with him," she confessed.

After Marianne left, Ruby—shocked by her sister's story—sat on the living room couch in a trance. *Why would Jason do that?* She desperately tried to mentally work through the comments about Jason's behaviour.

Recently, Ruby had read an article in a woman's magazine about people who are addicted to sex—sex in the broadest terms. She wondered if any of this new information could explain Jason's behaviour. She was certain she must research this topic further.

She started putting together some other details. Recently, she had become aware of some other odd changes in Jason's behaviour. He had secrets, she was sure. She became more suspicious of his increased and very late overtime hours.

Ruby knew she needed answers. She had to talk to Jason. His unfaithfulness hurt a lot. His anger and abusive behaviour was something Ruby needed to deal with. She thought that she must get a handle on what she did to cause him to be so angry. Right or wrong, Ruby believed in her marriage vows. The words her mother said to her when she announced her pregnancy still occupied a place in her brain. Ruby vowed she would make her marriage work. Should the marriage stop working, she must not end up on welfare, as her mother had predicted.

Ruby practiced for several hours planning how she could have the discussion with Jason about his behaviour with Marianne.

Ruby tried to tactfully broach the subject with him. "I guess you've noticed that Marianne's not available to look after Matt these days."

"No. I haven't."

"Do you have any idea why?"

"Nope. I don't have a clue. I guess she's off getting laid by her boyfriend. Maybe she's just lost interest in Matt," he flippantly responded.

"Funny, she seems to think that you acted inappropriately the last few times that you drove her home." She tried to not actually accuse Jason of any wrongdoing.

She didn't succeed. Ruby was shocked as she watched the scene develop right in front of her as if she was watching a movie. His wild overreaction to what he interpreted as an accusation was beyond any reasonable expectation. He flew into a violent rage. His bullying behaviour once again appeared out of nowhere. He approached Ruby with his fist in the air, ready to connect with her body while he adamantly denied Marianne's allegations. "Don't you ever, *ever* accuse me of having any interest in your dumb little sister again."

He was both verbally and physically abusive. With wide eyes that looked like they would pop out of their sockets and a face beet red like he might explode any minute, he started yelling and screaming at Ruby. He shrieked, "You stupid bitch. Why would you believe that little bitch over me? I'm your husband, for God's sake. Marianne is a tramp. Get wise to your little sister."

"Please, can we just have a calm conversation?"

"Yes, if you could just stop accusing me instead of asking."

"Jason, I'm trying to …"

"You are such a stupid bitch. Why don't you just shut up?"

He then proceeded to push Ruby into the wall with his body. He pressed his hands hard against her chest and forearms. Fear that he would someday do her serious harm and the almost unbearable pain to Ruby's already bruised body made her wince and pull away.

When it was over, he yelled over his shoulder, "Get out of my house, you useless piece of shit." With that, he left the house and slammed the door behind him.

Ruby was alone—bruised, crying and trying to figure out what had just happened and what she could have done differently.

Chapter 13

Tenth Wedding Anniversary, January 13 1966

Rock and roll music from the sixties blasted from the radio and later from the stereo playing vinyl records. Ruby's favourite singers that she cherished—like the Beatles, Elvis Presley, the Platters and the Crew Cuts—made the work fun. She sang and danced while she cleaned the house and prepared for their special anniversary dinner. She was oozing with both hope and energy today.

She felt really good about herself, her marriage and her relationship with Jason. Her mood was so much better when Jason was also in a good mood and reasonably pleasant. She didn't know why, so she decided not to question him, as this could set him off on one of his angry abusive rages. She was happy to believe they were past the bad times.

She was sure he would like what she had cooked. She'd used his Italian mother's secret recipe for pasta fagioli al forno. It was always a lot of work, but this Italian-inspired dish of baked pasta with beans had become his favourite meal. The sauce needed to be cooked the whole day at a very low temperature, but it was always worth it. She knew this meal would put him in a great frame of mind and make him happy.

Ruby wanted everything to be perfect, so she took the time to double-check everything. She critically looked over the table, making sure it was set with a freshly ironed white tablecloth, cloth napkins, good china, wineglasses, salad plates and bread and butter plates—just like he always insisted. She reached down and adjusted a butter knife that had gone askew. Perfect!

It was important that she review the multiple pieces of cutlery she had set out, making sure they were appropriately placed around the table setting. She leaned over and smiled. A colourful mixed bouquet of fresh flowers was centered between two tall tapered white candles. The presentation of the table suggested a very special dinner. The scent of the flowers caused her to beam, as the perfect picture pleased her. It was her best effort in a very long time.

Just then, the phone rang. Her heart sank. *I hope that isn't Jason telling me that he has been detained.*

It was Jason. "Happy anniversary, sweetie," he said. "I'll be home in about twenty minutes. I'm stuck in traffic. There seems to be a holdup at the bridge over River Street. See you soon."

"Hurry home," she said. "I don't want our dinner to spoil. Bye for now."

Hanging up the phone, Ruby smoothed out her apron and then turned to once again admire her perfectly set table. She smiled and praised herself because she had put a lot of effort into this dinner. She was convinced it was going to be the best anniversary meal. She was happy that her mom was able to keep the children overnight. *Who knows what we might get up to?* A mischievous smirk appeared on her face, as if she was enjoying the most wonderful orgasm that she was anticipating for herself later that evening.

Drawing her bath, she poured in her favourite scented bath oil with a wonderful spicy vanilla fragrance. Jason had told her many times how much this oil, in particular, turned him on. She eased herself into the warm water with lots of bubbles. She took the time to enjoy the luxurious sensual feeling of the gentle jets of water from her whirlpool tub. She was relaxed and smelled delicious enough to eat. *I hope Jason will be in a sexy mood too.*

She gently towel-dried her now very horny body, dusted it with fragrant vanilla body powder, then lightly misted her body with the same scent of cologne. *Not too much now, just enough. This will set the mood.*

She flossed and brushed her teeth. She didn't want bad breath, because this would turn off Jason. With hair dried and styled and a touch of makeup, she was ready.

What will I wear? she asked herself as she flipped through her leisure dresses hanging in her closet. Her eyes and hands passed over several lounging types. As soon as her hand touched the silky soft sensual fabric of her red one, she knew instantly that this was it. Quickly, but with special attention to details, she slipped into the floor-length fire-engine-red dress. The skirt was full enough to swirl and slide around her hips. She chose to not wear underwear. She liked the way the fabric swished against her bare skin when she walked. Best of all, it sensually exposed her cleavage. This dress had always been Jason's favourite.

Jason opened the front door and hollered, "I'm home! Sure does smell great in here." With the rustling sound of Ruby's dress, he looked up the stairs and was taken aback at the image of Ruby descending, a fantasy in scarlet. "Well, well, hello, my sexy lady!" he smiled, revealing his pleasure at the sight.

Ruby, pleased with the greeting she had hoped for, ran to him, put her arms around his neck and passionately kissed him. "Welcome home, honey. I made your favourite meal—homemade pasta fagioli al forno, salad and garlic bread."

"I know! I could smell it before I opened the door. Mmm-mm. Can we eat soon?" he asked. "I'm getting hungry. The aroma is making my taste buds work overtime, just anticipating how great this meal is going to taste."

"Sure. It's all done. You can pour us a glass of wine while I put dinner together," Ruby said, smiling back at him as she walked toward the kitchen. "I'm the happiest I've been in a very long time," she added with a broad smile while looking over her shoulder toward Jason.

"I'll wash up, and then I'll open the wine," he softly uttered on his way to the bathroom.

Walking back into the dining room, he complimented her. "The table looks great, sweetie. I love that you're using the good china for our special dinner. You really have worked very hard today. This place looks so clean, we could eat off the floor. I realize you also worked all day preparing our meal. Thanks."

Jason was praising Ruby. This was not his normal behaviour, but he did seem to be in a particularly good mood. Maybe she was finally pleasing him. Ruby secretly congratulated herself.

Jason poured two glasses of wine. He put her glass on the kitchen counter so she could sip it while she creatively arranged the dinner on the plates.

"Jason, please light the candles, and then have a seat. Dinner's ready," she softly announced. "I purposely chose your favourite wine, valpolicella, for our anniversary," she said as she approached the table. "The children are having a sleepover at Mom's, so we have the house to ourselves—all night." She grinned in her most flirtatious manner. *I hope he got the hint that I'm horny and looking for great sex tonight.* Ruby was sure the evening was going to be wonderfully romantic.

Out of Silence

She did wonder why was there was no flirting or pats on the bum like usual. Jason seemed preoccupied. *It must be just my imagination working overtime. Come on, Ruby,* she coached herself, *it's probably nothing. Don't be reading things into a comment and spoil a pleasant evening,* she scolded herself. She did wonder, though.

She was pleased that they did playfully flirt a little while they slowly drank wine and leisurely ate the prized meal. They chatted about the family and the daily events at Jason's work.

When their gourmet meal and Jason's favourite dessert, crème caramel, were finished, however, he pushed himself away from the table and announced, "I have to go out for a few hours. I won't be too long."

Ruby sat there with shock written all over her face. She asked, "Where are you going? I thought …"

Jason interrupted her. "Don't start." He didn't even let her finish her sentence. "Just out," he stated abruptly, with a slight agitation in his voice.

"But Jason, it's our anniversary. Can't you change your plans?" she asked, now showing her disappointment with *his* change of *her* plans.

"Here you go again. Nag, nag, nag," he spat.

"When did this appointment come up? You didn't mention it this morning or when we spoke just before dinner." She knew she was pushing, but she wanted answers.

"Look, I told you, I'll only be a couple of hours. Why can't you accept what I say and get off my back?" he snapped. He never wanted to defend his actions.

"Jason, I just don't understand. I want to, really. But I don't. Just tell me who is your appointment with? That's all." She was getting very suspicious. Those old feelings of jealousy were pushing to the surface.

"It's none of your damn business. I said I'm going out. That's final. See, you always do this. You spoil everything. This is just like you. We had a great dinner, and now you've spoiled the mood."

"Why won't you tell me? Are you seeing someone? Just tell me." She knew questioning him was not a good idea, but right now, she didn't care. She was more concerned about her own feelings. "I really do want to know. At the very least, I'm entitled to an explanation." A feeling of abandonment swept over her entire body.

Jason stood up abruptly, knocking over his chair. As it slammed to the floor, with determination he walked to the kitchen counter and chose one of the large carving knives. Knife in hand, he returned to the dining area and pointed the knife at Ruby. "I do not have to explain my comings and goings to you. You did a good job with the dinner, thanks. But you have just overstepped your bounds."

"What do you mean? What bounds? What are you talking about? More importantly, what are you going to do with that knife?" Ruby was very worried now. Quickly she got to her feet. She was conscious of putting a barrier, the table, between them.

He glared at her with a look of distaste, like he was being forced to eat something he didn't like. "I would really like to put you out of your misery, once and for all. You are just so stupid. Just ask me one more question, and it will be your last. I promise. Stupid bitch," he screamed while waving around the knife.

"Jason, put down that knife, please," she pleaded. "I won't ask any more questions. Just go and do whatever it is you need to do."

"It's too late for that now. You just won't shut up, will you? You go on and on pushing and pushing," he yelled, his anger reaching a fever pitch. His face now turned crimson with his raised blood pressure. He jabbed the knife in the air, pretending to swipe at her.

Is this how he kills me? I'm so afraid, more than ever before. I'm in fear for my life.

He quickly moved to his left. Ruby darted to move quickly to her left. He shuffled again to his right. Ruby countered his move by putting more distance between them. It was like a dance of warriors, he with a clashing sabre. The problem was, Ruby didn't have a sabre.

She was unsure of how long she could successfully fend him off. This was her worst nightmare. He was really frightening her right now.

Jason appeared to be ready for a fight. His anger had escalated in a split second, and he was out of control. Once and for all, he would show her that it was not her place to question his whereabouts. The blade of the knife flashed as it caught the light of the candles. Each time he waved or thrust it in her direction, he came closer and closer. Several times, he feigned jabbing her with the sharp blade. He appeared more dangerous than she had ever experienced in the past.

Ruby sobbed. Tears were now streaming down her face. He had threatened her with a knife previously. That time, she only suffered minor cuts. *I must calm him down. How? What will work this time?*

"Jason, can you please just stop this jostling? I promise to not question you again. Please put that knife down. I admit, I'm quite terrified. No one is going to feel good about this tomorrow morning, especially if one of us gets hurt." *I'm pretty sure that someone will be me. It is always me.*

He had plans, so he needed to stop this little battle. But she knew from past incidents that he would only stop if he was the victor. He wanted her to beg and plead. This gave him the power that he craved and was essential for him.

"Please, Jason. Put the knife down. You go. Do what you need to do. I will clean up the table and the kitchen. Please, just go."

For a few seconds, Ruby let her guard down, and he reached across the table and jabbed at her with the kitchen knife. He finally made contact. They both watched as the point of the knife drew blood on her forearm.

Ruby screamed, "Stop. Jason, stop. I'm bleeding." The blood dropped onto the white tablecloth. "I need to get cleaned up. Please, just go."

Jason took this as a win. He put the knife down and said, "We'll deal with this later. I have someplace to be." With that, he walked to the door, picked up his coat and keys and slammed the door shut behind him, shaking the whole house.

Relieved, Ruby sat down and cried. She carefully wrapped a soiled napkin around her arm, tying it off like a tourniquet. The bleeding stopped in a few minutes. She regained her composure and then washed and bandaged her arm correctly, hoping to stop the bleeding and that the slash would not leave a scar. She knew she wasn't being realistic about that.

Mumbling away to herself, she cleared the dishes from the table, set the upended chair erect and washed the last bits of food from the dirty pots, pans and dishes. After putting food into containers and into the refrigerator, Ruby loaded the dishes into the dishwasher.

So much for the sexy "Happy anniversary, dear!" she mimicked on her way to the bedroom. She picked up the pink satin and lace negligée that had been carefully and strategically placed on the bed. With disgust, Ruby tossed the garment to the floor. She didn't need or want a reminder of her failed plan for their sexy evening. Totally exhausted both physically and emotionally, Ruby quickly fell into a deep sleep.

She woke up with a start at the sound of a noise coming from somewhere in the house. Looking over at his empty side, she realized he had not come to bed. Checking the alarm clock, she saw that it was now well after midnight. *Where did he go? Why isn't he home yet?*

Ruby was laying there reviewing the events of the evening in her head when she heard Jason stumble into the bedroom, bumping into the foot of the bed. She glanced at the clock on the nightstand. *Where has he been until two in the morning?*

She thought, *He didn't demand sex. This is good. But why*? She sniffed the air and closed her eyes. *I don't really need to ask that question. I hate the smell of that sickly pungent scent of sex from someone else.* She got a whiff of stale perfume. *Definitely not a fragrance I would use. Now I'm sure that he has been with another woman. Again!*

Chapter 14

Married Fourteen Years Now

One time, their fourteen-year-old son, Matt, watched and cried, "Dad, let Mommy go. Dad, please don't hurt Mommy."

Jason spat, "Go to bed. Get out of here. Go to your room and close the door." When he tired of abusing her, he left her bruised body on the floor like a pile of crumpled clothing.

During this period, Ruby often cried until her tear ducts ran dry. She sank deeper and deeper into depression. She became an introvert with strong feelings of inferiority. At the same time, she wondered if she could get away with killing him. She was desperate, but not that desperate, yet ... so she quickly kicked that thought out of her head. That was not a viable solution. No one would ever have described Ruby as a violent person. She made up her mind that she would not sink to his level.

She was so unhappy, and Jason refused to talk to her or explain. Why did he act like such a horrible monster?

Eventually, he'd calm down and say, "Sorry, Ruby. I won't do that again, because I really do love you." Then he'd add, "You make me do things to you that I regret. I never want to hurt you. It's just that you make me so mad at you, 'cause you say such stupid mean things."

Jason would hold her and gently kiss her face, neck and breasts. He would apologize again, and then he'd ask her to try harder to please him. These makeup sessions normally ended in sexual intercourse. He called it making love. She didn't agree, but she knew better than to openly disagree with him. She feared this would send him into another round of more severe abusive behaviour.

Ruby Monroe

She convinced herself that if she really worked at pleasing him and kept her opinions to herself, he would stop the abuse. She promised herself that she could do this. She knew she could. She had to try.

Ruby had determined that special days and holidays seemed to set him off. Most long weekends were occasions for an episode of abuse. Why?

The bruises on her body were never visible to their families or her coworkers. If they were aware of her changing character or her physical bruises and the psychological abuse she endured, they never mentioned it to her. Thank goodness, as she wouldn't know how to explain it and keep her self-respect. Of course, she would never broach the subject, as it was far too embarrassing and humiliating—and, most important, she was ashamed that she'd let a man treat her like a punching bag. She would tell anyone who questioned her, "If you haven't walked a mile in an abused person's shoes, don't judge." How could anyone possibly understand an abused person's pitiful life?

Ruby had read an article recently that made her wonder if she might have something like Stockholm syndrome. There was no doubt in her mind that she was Jason's prisoner and personal punching bag. At this time, it never occurred to her that it was his problem, not hers. The only way she could continue to be with family and friends and go to work was to compartmentalize her moods and demeanour. It became easier as time moved on.

Ruby had once been a smart, happy, outgoing young woman, but her self-esteem had been systematically destroyed. She found it harder and harder to act like her old self. She scarcely ever laughed anymore. She couldn't find humour in any situation.

She knew something had to be done to change the direction in which her life was heading. But how can that happen when you're not allowed to speak to anyone—family, doctor, or friends—about what goes on behind closed doors? How do you find help? When your life and your children's lives are threatened, how do you get away from *him?*

Ruby kept her head down at home. She had learned which behaviours of hers didn't upset Jason. She performed the duties of her job, and with several upgrades and promotions, earned excellent money. This lifted her morale and demeanour. Now she wanted a better life.

As human resources manager, she counselled a few women who were abused by their partner and wanted to get help or divorced. Ruby searched for resources for battered and abused women. She learned that these places were in short supply—plus the outcome for the women who used them were not always positive.

During her research, Ruby learned that unfortunately, calling the police for the most part didn't have the desired outcome. Most abused women were afraid to make formal complaints due to the bullying guarantees that their partner, husband, or boyfriend made if law enforcement was contacted. The male abuser was calm until the officers left, and then the abuse continued. In another scenario, the abuser might be removed from the home, but after a night in jail, he went home angrier than ever—angry enough to kill.

Chapter 15

1971: Married for Fifteen Years

Ruby was driving to work after the particularly nasty smack-down drag-out fight with Jason that followed the party at Lloyd and Susan's house. Jason drove the wrong direction toward oncoming traffic on the way home, nearly causing a serious accident, and he had followed that up with rape. The next morning, he had approached Ruby, grabbed her arm and repeated his angry comment from the night before: "You know, you really are a cold fish, Ruby. I do wonder why I waste my time on you."

She couldn't get over the feeling of being discarded like a useless piece of clothing after he raped her again last night. She felt worthless and abused.

Ruby yearned to be free of the monster she'd married. *How could I have ever thought that I loved him? I hate him so much. If only he would just go away. Will I ever be free of his abuse? Why does he always make me the guilty one?*

She'd cried herself to sleep, wishing she was dead. She knew she never wanted to feel like that again. That morning, Ruby couldn't get out of the house fast enough. She had to get to work and didn't want another physical encounter with Jason.

She was sure that she was going to have a mental breakdown soon. How much longer could she pretend all was well? That was what she was doing: *pretending.* Ruby was now convinced that it was time to consult a lawyer. She needed legal advice. She and her husband shared investments, property and children. She didn't think for a minute that their two sons would ever entertain the thought of living with their father; in addition to abusing her, he had at times over-disciplined or abused them. In fact, their sons had already moved out. They couldn't take it anymore. It was important now that she understand her rights.

Ruby made two promises to herself. First, she would not spend the rest of her life with that animal she married. Second, she had worked hard to achieve her managerial position, and she would not let that be taken away from her. But how do you get free from someone who has threatened your life and your children's lives several times? Jason had frequently threatened that if she ever attempted to leave him, he would kill them all.

Yes, advice from a lawyer is definitely what I need, and soon.

About ten minutes into her drive, she could no longer hold back the flood of tears. She cried so hard that her body convulsed with shuddering sobs. It wasn't a long journey to the next town where she had worked as human resources manager for the past two years, but today the trip seemed to take an eternity.

Normally she enjoyed the pleasant relaxing scenery of large farms and fields that produced vegetables and feed for the farm animals. She loved the old interesting farmhouses, some in better repair than others. Usually, she played a game with herself, trying to guess what the people who lived in these houses looked like and especially how they had or had not decorated their historical homes.

Today she saw very little of the scenery through her tears. *Stop! Get a hold of yourself,* she scolded. The screaming and arguing that morning had taken up most of her energy and time. Eating breakfast and performing her regular morning chores had been difficult. She'd had no time to spare after what seemed like a never-ending fight with Jason followed by his abusive behaviour.

She wondered why he picked the busiest time of her day to find fault and demand that she do things for him. Whenever he didn't get his way or she didn't respond quickly enough, he started shoving and pushing her around. This made her preparation for work rushed and very unpleasant. She found it difficult to mentally focus on work or home when she was in this state of mind. From articles she had read, she thought their little family might be a textbook definition of *dysfunctional*.

She knew she couldn't sport red-rimmed eyes from crying when she arrived at the office. She was a manager, and managers don't cry. She finally got control of her feelings, and this stopped the tears. Ruby turned her focus back to her work.

Through long practice, she knew how to compartmentalize her life. It was important to put times like this morning away. She must not think about the past three hours while at work. She mentally prepared herself for the duties and scheduled meetings today at the office.

Ruby pulled into her designated parking space. She looked in the rear-view mirror to reassure herself before she exited her car. It was necessary to make sure that she had put on her business face and happy demeanour. While at the office she was an actress—and a good one at that—no matter what had happened to her since she left the office the day before. She buried all that or checked it at the company front door. With her business face and easygoing, caring personality, she was ready for another day at the office.

Ruby had quit high school at 16, so she lacked the formal education usually required for a management position. She had studied and worked hard to acquire her professional credentials. She had earned this job. The climb up the corporate ladder had not been easy. For some reason, men preferred to hire men. She had read and observed that this was more about the jock talk in interviews with men than their qualifications, especially when men were interviewed by men.

During her more junior years, she had overheard her own supervisor's conversations during his male interviews. That was exactly how the interviews began—with last weekend's football game or whichever sport they found common ground over. She observed that even though few men had developed the soft skills required to deal with personnel issues, some were very successful in this area. But there were far more successful females in the various human resources positions that involved direct contact with employees.

Ruby knew she had to constantly remind herself that when she finally left Jason, she would need her managerial position and her respectable salary more than ever. She had to continue to enhance her skills with courses and conferences. She wanted to be competent in her chosen field. This is what kept her motivated.

Chapter 16

1972: Married Sixteen Years

Work at her current employer—an envelope manufacturing company, Grange Envelopes—continued to go well for Ruby. Due to her hard work, she was rewarded with another move up the corporate ladder. She earned good money and was promoted to a new position with additional responsibilities. She kept on compartmentalizing her life.

Every morning, during her drive or ride on public transportation, she mentally moved or changed her thinking about herself to suit the destination. This was how she survived. At work, no one knew about her home life, and she didn't want to share it with anyone. That would be too humiliating. During business hours and at business functions, she was well adjusted, happy and very qualified to do her job. She earned the respect of managers and employees alike.

The employees really liked her. How refreshing and gratifying that was for Ruby. She felt hope creeping into her mind.

Ruby was flattered by the attention of Ron Battle. She became infatuated with him. He was kind to her and treated her like an equal. It didn't hurt that he was a very intelligent, successful guy. She liked his casual manner and his slightly mischievous smile. It turned her on. His great looks really appealed to Ruby.

I spend more time thinking about Ron than any man I have ever known, she thought. *I think he is perfectly beautiful. His wife is so lucky. What I wouldn't do to have someone with his strength and disposition loving me. Those clear blue eyes and curly blonde hair make me hold my breath when we meet in the halls. Like a schoolgirl with a crush, I stumble over my words. I'm sure he thinks I'm an idiot.*

Ron had the kind of athletic body that most men would love to have. He was 6 feet 2 inches tall, with broad shoulders and narrow hips. He wore smart modern business suits that enhanced his firm body. Crisp white shirts and colourful ties completed the picture. For some reason, Ruby found his business attire so very sensual.

Ron frequently complimented her. He was always attentive and often sat at her table in the cafeteria during lunch or coffee breaks. Ruby learned that Ron was drawn to her because she, like him, held an important managerial position. They worked together on a committee, evaluating salary positions and determining levels of compensation. For this reason, no one thought anything of or was suspicious about their casual meetings. They innocently flirted for a few months. It was fun and so good for her ego. He treated her with kindness and respect.

Following months of teasing and joking around, they decided to act on their physical attraction. One day during their coffee break, he broached the subject. He lowered his head as if telling her a secret. "Ruby, I have a friend who lives in an apartment close to our offices over on Branson Street. I asked him if he would be amenable to letting me use his apartment during lunchtime. Just a couple of days would be great. What do you think?"

"Oh my God, Ron, you didn't tell him who you would be with, did you?" Ruby asked in a panic. *What if Jason found out? It would be the worst day of my life—maybe the last.*

"No, of course I didn't. He's cool. You know, he's a guy. We do things like this for each other." Ron sought to set aside any fear of recognition Ruby might be feeling.

"Okay, as you are also very aware, this little meeting is just for sex, and it would not help either one of us professionally if our secret was discovered." She felt she needed to set the parameters up front. She tried to be very careful and hoped they could continue to be as anonymous as possible.

Ruby remembered something she had read. It struck her as if someone was describing her situation: "Women have affairs to escape their life." She didn't know the author, but it was uncanny how it fit her motivation and alibi for the extramarital sex she was about to become involved in.

In the beginning, they couldn't get to the apartment fast enough. While in the elevator, they fumbled with buttons so they could quickly remove each other's clothing once behind closed doors. They kissed until their lips were sore. Ruby developed a rash on her cheek and upper lip from his stubbly face. It was truly amazing. Their emotions rose to heights neither one had previously experienced. They gave each other truly great, mind-blowing, passionate sex.

Every time, his large erect penis sent her to the most wonderful pinnacles of pleasure. When she finally landed, she sighed with total contentment. Jokingly, she congratulated Ron on his excellent performance. She lay there all warm and mushy inside, enjoying the many aftershocks that always followed her intense orgasms. It was the most wonderful feeling.

Who needs drugs when you have orgasms in your arsenal? she asked herself. *This tryst with Ron is great for my self-esteem and has helped build up my battered ego. This is what life should be like. I feel like a totally different person these days.*

It was just sex. They both knew it. But it was absolutely spectacular sex. *Maybe the attraction is stronger due to it being the forbidden fruit,* she thought. *I don't know, and at this point, I really don't care. I want to be with him as often as we can sneak away.*

Sometimes it was almost impossible to walk normally around the office after their nooner. Her legs felt weak and unstable, like they would give way and she'd fall to the floor. She knew the wonderful sensation was the product of their magnificent sexual encounters. She kind of enjoyed the rubber legs, because it felt like the sensation was being prolonged and remembered longer in both her mind and body.

They explored each other's bodies with their hands, lips and tongues, kissing and caressing, finding the arousal spots that brought the other one to a wonderful soul-filling mind-blowing exciting climax. *Who is this woman wearing my clothes—or in this case, no clothes?* She was only there when they were alone and having raunchy sex, Ruby observed, noting the change in her personality. *Ron is therapy for my soul, frame of mind and sense of well-being.*

This new, more confident Ruby was being noticed at work, too. Her boss, Mr. Gaines, must have noticed, as he was giving her tougher assignments. For the first time in a very long time, she felt great and self-confident.

Ron and Ruby walked to his friend's apartment at noon a couple of days each and every week for several months. It took Ruby four visits to their love nest before she noticed the decor of his friend's apartment. She speculated that Ikea was doing well, and the apartment owner was very handy with building tools.

Eventually, their hot and heavy passionate nooners, although still hot, became less and less frequent. They both agreed to terminate the affair, as the excitement and anticipation had faded somewhat. She concluded they were lucky to not have been caught. Ruby no longer needed the therapy. They did remain friends and continued for several more months to work professionally on several committees with a team of their peers. But they never returned to their hot sex bed in the apartment of the anonymous landlord.

Chapter 17
1973: Finally Proof

At home, things went from bad to worse. Ruby was looking for a specific amount of an item they had purchased because she wanted to return it. She knew it had been charged to their Visa credit card. While inspecting the monthly statements, she noticed a one-time charge at a motel. She checked the Yellow Pages directory for the address. To her surprise, it was only a twenty-minute drive from their house. She knew she had never stayed there, and Jason would not need to stay there on business; he could just drive home.

Her curiosity was piqued. She continued to scrutinize the previous month's statements. It showed three more charges at the same motel. Getting more angry, she continued looking back over six more months, and she was shocked to find more and more charges. The dates were different, but it was always at the same motel. She felt a gnawing sharp pain in the pit of her stomach and wondered, *What's going on here. Are these fraudulent charges?*

She called the bank. Intuitively, Ruby knew what she would find out. She just didn't want to believe what was already evident. The credit card representative didn't see a pattern that would throw up a red flag for these being fraudulent charges. It was determined that the charges were probably authentic.

She tried to not jump to conclusions just yet, but she couldn't deny the facts: Jason was having another affair. No wonder money was tight. He was spending their hard-earned money on his casual affairs.

She did feel pangs of guilt, as only recently she was physically involved with Ron. She and Jason were not having sex these days. He had someone else—but for a short time, so had she. Did that make it right for either one of them? Absolutely not! But she couldn't help remembering the great feelings she had while making love with Ron. She couldn't deny it. It was lovely.

Ruby had never previously sought out proof of Jason's indiscretions, but she decided that for her peace of mind and possibly proof that might be needed if the divorce went to court, she had to investigate. The motel charges were pushing her. Deep down, she didn't want to have concrete evidence, because then she would have to actually divorce Jason. She wasn't ready to go there just yet, but it had become very difficult to have a normal conversation with him. She had to build her case by gathering this evidence.

A few days later, with that nagging feeling in the pit of her stomach, she drove to the motel. She expected the worst, and she wasn't disappointed. The place was a dump. Still somewhat in denial, she thought, *Why would Jason bring anyone here?* She walked into the dingy office with a strange musty odour that seemed to get caught in her throat. She asked for information about the charges on the statement from the scraggly unkempt toothless elderly man sitting behind the counter. She crinkled her nose, associating the odour with urine or someone who hadn't bathed in some time. The horrible smell of the office made her feel ill.

She'd had the forethought to bring a photo of Jason with her. Deep inside her mind, she no longer suspected him of indiscretions; she knew. She held up the picture and asked the front desk clerk, "Have you ever seen this person here at this motel?"

Without hesitation, the desk clerk said, "Yep! He and his wife or friend check in here for an afternoon or evening at least once a week. Why?" he asked. "What's your interest? Who are you anyway?"

As calmly as she could, she mustered her strength and composure and then responded, "His wife."

The hotel clerk had a look on his face indicating his uneasiness.

"I'm sorry to bother you. Thank you for the information." She knew she had to do something. She had to get out of there. Her mind flashed with scenarios of him in bed with a cheap floozie, cheating on his wife. *What kind of woman would have casual sex in this dump? He has really hit rock bottom.*

She rushed home and checked the beds for bugs. How dare he be so careless?

She knew now that nothing she said or did was ever going to be good enough for him. He continued to hurt her even when he wasn't in the room. She felt humiliated and betrayed.

As much as she dreaded the confrontation, she decided it was time to deal with Jason. She knew he would be angry with her.

A few nights later, they were in the family room watching a hockey game. During a commercial, she casually said, "Jason, the other day I was looking for a charge on our Visa and noticed a few charges for a motel I know I have never stayed at …" That was all she got out of her mouth.

He immediately flew into a rage, shoving and punching her.

"Please, Jason, stop hitting me. I will not be your personal punching bag."

"You will be whatever I decide you are. Don't tell me what I can and can't do. Stupid bitch!" Jason shouted disparaging and cruel insults about her and her lack of interest in sex and him. He screamed, "I only see these women because I need to get it elsewhere, as you're useless in bed."

Ruby was puzzled by his ranting. His comments about sex or lack thereof were, as usual, unwarranted. *Here we go again.*

"Your job is to take care of the kids and the house. Do your damn job and shut up."

"You blame me and make me feel like everything that goes wrong, including your indiscretions, is my fault." She didn't know where this boldness came from, but it felt good. She was the victim, and he would pay.

He continued to curse and yell at her. He turned to her as if a new idea struck him, and then he said, "Why are you looking at things on my desk anyway? Everything in there is in the none-of-your-business department. Just stay out of my desk."

Ruby got up to walk away, but he grabbed her and turned her around facing him. He pushed up against her with his now larger beer belly and began yelling. His face was so close to hers when he shouted that she felt a wet spray on her face from his saliva. He slammed her into the basement cement wall with such force that he knocked the wind out of her. He slammed her again into the wall really hard, again and again, until she lay crumpled on the floor, sobbing with pain and humiliation. When she attempted to get to her feet, he yanked her up by her sweater and shoved her into the wall again.

"Please, Jason, I was just asking. Stop! Jason, please don't do that. You're hurting me," she pleaded.

Ruby escaped to her bedroom. He did not follow.

The next morning, Ruby was once again bruised and sore from being knocked around. She was mentally and physically hurting. He had made her feel at fault, as usual. He had a way of turning things around and blaming her for his nasty outbursts.

After that episode, the desk was always locked.

She thought about getting professional help but wouldn't feel right going to a counsellor. She was afraid to be asked the most obvious questions: "Why now? Why did you put up with his bad behaviour for so long?" She was too embarrassed, and her self-esteem hit an all-time low.

What had she done to deserve this monster? Marriage vows obviously meant nothing to him. Maybe the part "Until death do you part" was more real than she had ever dreamed.

Recently she had read an article about sexually transmitted diseases. *What about me? How can I protect myself from these diseases?* She had lots of unanswered questions. *I do wonder if he wears a condom when he's with these other women.*

Ruby booked an appointment with her personal physician to be tested for STDs.

Chapter 18

1976: Married Twenty Years

Jason was doing very well at work. Recently he had been promoted to manager of the internal audit team. This meant more travel than his previous position; now he was in charge of a team of accountants with the responsibility for auditing the books of his company's many branches.

Jason often stayed at distant hotels when he was away on his five-day financial audits. He frequently ate alone at very nice restaurants. His favourite was a family-run Italian place. He became very friendly with the owners. Antonio, waiter and owner of Authentic Italian Fine Foods, introduced Jason to pork spare ribs that had been cooked in the spaghetti sauce for many hours by his little old Italian mother. This was a family-only special meal.

Jason was single during these trips.

He bragged to Ruby about how the owner and the mother treated him like family. He also shared with Ruby that the mother made him their family's favourite meal. Jason was very happy, but Ruby was jealous.

A few years later, she discovered that during these business trips, he frequently brought women he met at the restaurant to his hotel room for sex. It didn't matter how frequently he committed adultery, it always felt like another slap in the face.

During this calmer period, things were much better at home. Even the beatings had ceased. Civility once again was the norm. She mentally crossed her fingers and hoped this truce held longer than the last one.

Ruby felt more confident about their relationship for the first time in many years. She felt that they were over the hump. Her job was also going very well. She attended night school to bring up her grades, as she now had researched the requirements to become a registered nurse—her dream job. Her research uncovered information about a local college that offered mature student nurse's training. This was exciting news, as due to her pregnancy at age 16, she had not graduated from high school, a normal requirement for becoming a registered nurse.

Ruby proudly wrote an emotional but factual letter about her lifelong desire to work in the nursing field. Included in the package were her reports showing that she had successfully upgraded her education in the required subjects. Every course showed not only completion with 100 percent attendance but also all As.

Much to her surprise and pleasure, she received an invitation to take a test for the training. She was so excited about this tremendous opportunity that it was difficult to concentrate at work. Finally, exam day arrived. The exams were held on a Saturday and Sunday in May. She wrote many general knowledge and psychological-type exams during two very long eight-hour days. Even though she was mentally spent, she felt like her feet weren't touching the ground. During her drive home, she sang along to the Judy Garland song on the radio, "I can't give you anything but love, baby."

Life was going to be good when she started nurse's training. Jason would respect her when she graduated. All that crap and abuse would be behind them. She so wanted to believe that. In her heart, though, she knew better. People don't change.

When you are told often enough that you're worthless, you begin to believe it. She put up with and tolerated his miserable behaviour for so long, she was sure he would kill her before she would get up enough gumption to leave him. One might wonder why it took so long for Ruby to make her move and leave. She had been slowing working up the nerve to be free.

Chapter 19

Early May 1976: The Turning Point

Ruby received the long-awaited results of her registered nurse's exam. She held the small white envelope next to her heart and said a silent prayer: *I so hope I didn't fail. If I don't open it, I can't be disappointed.* With her heart racing and thumping like it was trying to escape from her chest, Ruby sat in the living room on her favourite love seat for fifteen minutes. She just rested there and stared at the unopened envelope, willing it to be an acceptance for the School of Nursing. *I'm afraid to open it, but I'm also afraid of not knowing what the letter might say. I need to have something positive happen. I have to open it.*

Her hands trembled as she slowly opened the flap. Taking the letter out and holding her breath, she read the words with dread. Then Ruby threw up her arms, held the letter up in the air and screamed, "Hurrah! I passed! I'm so happy. I passed!" The letter went on to say that she would be included in the upcoming September classes. She was ecstatic and on cloud nine. Being a nurse had been a dream of hers since she was seven or eight years old.

Ruby ran outside to where Jason was cutting the grass. "Jason," she called. "Look!" she waved the letter in the air, near his face to get his attention over the noise of the lawn mower. Excitedly she blurted out, "Jason, I've been accepted! I'll soon be a nurse—my dream job."

He looked at her with such disdain and said, "No. You can't afford to quit your job and go to school full-time. No. You *cannot* go."

It felt like he had poured a pail of ice water on her. Her high spirits and excitement were quickly doused. She was devastated by his totally negative and angry response. She didn't understand, so she asked, "Why did you let me go and take the tests if you already knew you were going to veto me quitting my job? I don't understand."

With disgust and hatred smeared all over his face like a mask, he sneered at her and said, "You stupid bitch. I didn't think that you were smart enough to pass. You just don't get it, do you?"

Even though she never did go for the nurse's training, just being accepted into the program gave her a huge psychological lift. She felt validated. She had been told so often that she was stupid, an idiot, a dumb bitch and more—but she now had been affirmed. She wasn't stupid after all.

Chapter 20

1978: Changes and Motivation

A couple of months later, Ruby was recruited away from her company to a new position at CCK, a manufacturer of creams and lotions, plus several other products used in the health-care industry. During her first week on the job, her boss, Mr. Wilson, gave her a recruitment assignment. She would be working with a bright young manager named George.

The two of them immediately hit it off. Ruby sensed that her office demeanour and looks pleased him. She liked him too. They became friendly business associates, often chatting and joking around during coffee breaks and lunches in the cafeteria.

She enjoyed his amusing, light-hearted and positive approach to problems. He always had an optimistic solution for any negative situation. She was drawn to him because he was different and a pleasing contrast to her husband's personality.

The first person she met on her way to the office on the second week at her new job was George. He had quickly become her escape from reality. He made her laugh no matter how deflated she felt inside her head. They flirted, joked and verbally teased each other. Smiling was easy when he was around. He made her feel like an attractive, fun person. If she was having a bad day and needed to bolster her self-esteem, she dropped by George's office.

That day, George sneaked up behind her and whispered close to her face, "Drop by my office later this morning. I have something I want to tell you."

Midmorning, after her coffee break, she stopped by George's office. The open-concept floor plan meant his office was really a managerial-size cubicle.

Ruby Monroe

In her position as human resources manager, she often met with managers to discuss their staffing issues. Therefore, stopping by George's office was normal.

She hesitated at the doorway, waiting for some direction from George, such as "wait," "come back later," or "have a seat." She could see that George seemed to be in a very serious telephone discussion with someone. He looked up and acknowledged her presence.

George had mentioned previously that he liked her friendly smile, the way she wore her short dark blonde hair and her blue eyes, as they were such a contrast to his large brown eyes. Ruby had cut her hair short just before starting her current position. Her slender body was more a result of not eating correctly or lack of appetite due to depression than a workout plan, but nonetheless, George had complimented her on her choices in business suits that revealed her slim curvy body.

George spoke into the receiver, again and again shrugging his shoulders in response to the person at the other end of the line. Ruby, studying George's face, saw him look directly at her. He gave her a big grin that exaggerated his cute dimples.

He then motioned to her to come in and sit down. With his hand over the mouthpiece, he said in a hushed voice. "Please sit. I won't be long."

Ruby parked herself in one the straight-backed visitor chairs. She was curious to hear what the intrigue was all about.

"Hello. Yes, I can do that. Tomorrow at three o'clock works for me. Thanks! See you then." He hung up the phone, put his hands together with fingers entwined and sadly looked across his desk. He appeared to be crushed, like he had stumbled across a serious problem, been given bad news, or had a shock.

She didn't know what to expect. She waited patiently for him to tell her. She saw the hurt in his eyes. Keeping her voice to just above a whisper, she asked, "What's wrong, George? Why are you so upset?"

"That was my lawyer. My wife left me on the weekend. Worst of all, she took our daughter, Tammy." He held back tears.

She observed that he was desperately trying to maintain his composure—mostly, she thought, because he was not ready to share his trauma with his staff and coworkers. When he looked up at her, she saw pools of tears filling his eyes. Those tears were in a holding pattern, just waiting to flood down his cheeks.

Filled with empathy, she said, "I'm so sorry, George. Is there anything I can do for you? Do you need time off? I'm sure you could use some personal time to deal with your very difficult situation. Maybe find a place to live?"

"Thanks. I did have the weekend to lick my wounds. I think I'm all cried out for now, anyway. I would like to ask a favour of you, though. As a friend, would you have a drink with me after work today?"

Silence hung over them like a blanket. Finally, she raised her eyebrows, expressing her surprise at the request. It was beyond the realm of their normal business relationship. Ruby hesitated for a moment and then said, "I don't know what to say. I don't want to give you the wrong impression. Maybe you should explain your agenda for a meeting after hours."

He assured her, "I just want to talk. This sounds selfish, but I would like to use you as a sounding board. I know you'll be impartial and keep everything I say strictly confidential, plus you are the best listener I know." He gave her a sheepish grin, hoping she would agree to the meeting.

"Okay, but I want to be very clear that we'll just be talking," Ruby stated, setting the ground rules and making sure she wasn't setting herself up for trouble.

"Thank you. I really appreciate you taking your personal time to be my friend. I thought we could meet at the Howard Johnson's bar near Ridley College around five o'clock. You agree that would be a good location?"

"You've spent some time planning this meeting."

"I've rehearsed how and what to say many times since Saturday."

"Why there?"

"It's at least a thirty-minute drive from work. We're not likely to meet or see anyone from work down in that area," George explained, taking charge of the situation. "Will you agree that the Howard Johnson's would be a good location?"

"Yes, that's a good location for a clandestine meeting. I can easily get to the highway and home quickly."

Walking back to her office, she admonished herself. *Ruby what are you doing? You know you're vulnerable right now. George is such a hunk.* She needed to stay focused. She wondered how this innocent conversation and meeting for drinks would impact their friendship and her marriage.

Chapter 21

1978: Plans Coming Together—or Disrupted?

Ruby went about her daily routine—calculating pensions and benefits and interviewing prospective employees. The interviews were great, as they helped keep her mind off her own personal issues. These duties required more intense concentration than the clerical duties. Her thoughts occasionally wandered onto personal subjects, such as George, divorce, lawyers and what she planned to do about each one of them.

She stopped at the receptionist desk where Shirley—an overweight, smartly dressed middle-aged woman with shoulder-length brown hair and hazel eyes—sat at her semicircular antique desk ready to greet guests. Ruby asked, "Shirley, I know that you live here in Markham just a couple of blocks away. Do you know offhand the name of a local family law solicitor? I prefer to make an appointment with someone who's known and can be recommended."

"Yes, as a matter of fact, I do. He was my divorce lawyer last year. He was great and very understanding," Shirley offered as she searched her personal address book for his listing. Shirley handed Ruby a yellow sticky note with his name and phone number written in pen. "Call him and tell him I referred you. He's great. I got to keep my kids. I think you will like him too."

Ruby accepted the sticky note, read the information, smiled and said, "Thanks so much. You're a lifesaver."

Inconspicuously as possible, she returned to her office and quietly closed the door. She didn't want an audience the one time she conducted personal business during working hours.

She took a moment to think of what she wanted to say before dialling the number. This was a major step for her, but she also thought a conversation with a lawyer was past due. Ruby gathered her thoughts and courage and then dialled the lawyer's number.

A receptionist answered the phone and announced in a very polite but businesslike tone, "Hello. Mr. Brown's office, family law specialists."

"Hi," said Ruby. "My name is Ruby Monroe. Our receptionist and a client of yours, Shirley Brant, referred me. I would like to book an appointment with Mr. Brown." Ruby hesitated, took a deep breath and then continued, "I think an appointment sooner rather than later would be best, if possible. I need to do this before I lose my nerve."

"I could slot you in this afternoon at 3:00 p.m. if that works for you, Ruby. For a new potential client, Mr. Brown offers one free consultation, so for today's visit there will be no charge."

"That's perfect. I'll see you at 3:00 p.m. Thanks." This was great, as she wouldn't need to spend any of her secret stash of money while investigating her options. Convinced that she'd only get one chance to make this move, she had no doubt that she must do it right the first time.

At 3:00 p.m. sharp, Ruby, with some reservations, entered the office of Mr. Brown, family law solicitor. It was located in a newer strip mall, but on the inside the attorney's offices looked serious and distinguished, with heavy wooden furniture and panel walls lined with legal books.

"Hello, Ruby. I'm Eric Brown," the solicitor said, offering his hand and shaking Ruby's. Eric was an elderly seasoned lawyer with green eyes, white hair and a slight build. Ruby wasn't sure if he was even five feet tall, as her five-foot-six-inch frame seemed to tower over him.

"Hello. Thank you for seeing me on such short notice." Ruby exhaled and took a deep breath before continuing. "I have to remind myself to breath." Her apprehension was obvious. "I want to leave my husband and felt the need to get some legal advice," Ruby blurted out as her voice quivered from built-up tension regarding her concern about the details she anticipated he would request and she would have to share, plus the advice he would give her. Right now, just making eye contact was very difficult. Being both nervous and embarrassed didn't help.

He paused, looked directly at Ruby and said, "I understand what you're asking is what do you need to know before you divorce your husband. Is that right?"

"Yes," she nervously responded as she squeezed her hands so hard she left fingerprints on the back of her other hand. She fidgeted in the oversized wooden chair.

"How long have you been married?"

"Almost twenty years."

"Do you have any children together?"

"Two boys. They no longer live at home."

During her free consultation, Mr. Brown gave her some tips on things she must get in order if she didn't want to lose everything to her husband. "First, I suggest that you obtain copies of your mortgage and status of payments, plus the balance. Secondly, make up a list of payments that you regularly make—credit card statements, your husband's pay stubs, bank statements and any other documents that would help when a settlement is discussed."

"I think I can get that information, though some may be difficult."

"Ruby, I don't know the circumstances, so I will tell you that if you leave the family home, you would be seen as abandoning the marriage, therefore putting yourself in jeopardy and in a negative position for the divorce process and custody of any children." He offered this advice as a warning to a very timid Ruby, who he saw wringing her hands and nervously squirming in the chair directly across from him.

Hearing these comments convinced Ruby to make the decision to divulge more details. "I must leave him because he is extremely abusive. The abusive behaviour and threats to kill me and my children make it impossible to continue to live in that house. Yet I'm terrified of leaving. He will kill me one day, either intentionally or because of an orchestrated accident, like being thrown down a flight of stairs or something like that. He's a monster."

Ruby paused to breathe and wipe her eyes. "Why can't I get away from him? Why?" she said, bringing more tears to her eyes. She had rushed through the information because of her shame and humiliation. Just saying it out loud to a stranger for the first time made her uncomfortable. She wondered, *Why should he believe me?*

"Wait a minute. You're telling me you're leaving due to his abusive behaviour?" he asked with wide eyes and a look of both compassion and determination on his face. "You definitely have my attention, and my advice to you in this situation is very different."

"Yes. I just can't take it anymore," she told him. "I have to get out. Neither one of our sons lives at home; they couldn't take it any longer. I need some advice about the house. We are both on the deed. We still have a small mortgage and owe a little money on credit cards."

"Take your time and try to relax. Breathe, Ruby, breathe," the lawyer calmly encouraged.

She took a couple of deep breaths. Feeling more relaxed now, she revealed Jason's threats. "Whenever I talk about leaving him, he threatens me. He says that he will kill me and the children. He says he will never allow me to leave him. Quite frankly, if it was just me, I would take the chance. But how does a mother put her children's lives on the line too?"

The concern for her situation showed on Mr. Brown's face. His body language told of his alarm, as he immediately sat up straight. He put his arms on the desk and leaned forward. "This alters my first advice for you. You still need the information. But I have some questions that you must consider also." He paused to make sure she was paying attention. "Have you ever called the police after one of these beatings?"

"No," she said in a whisper.

"Have you ever been treated in a hospital or by a doctor?"

"No." Once again, she spoke in a soft embarrassed tone.

"Have you made a complaint about the abuse to anyone—police, your family doctor or a friend?"

"No. You don't understand. That would send him into a rage, and I would likely be in for a very severe beating," she whispered again. She was worried. She realized that she was at a disadvantage for not reporting him previously. "How does one prove abuse if there is no evidence of abuse?"

"Did you know that you could go to one of the women's shelters? No questions asked," he informed her. He looked very troubled now.

Ruby hesitated before answering. Defensively, she responded, "I have heard of those shelters, but I don't think I qualify for them. I have a management job. Don't you need to be a charity case to be allowed into a shelter? Besides, he would never let me go."

"Who wouldn't let you go?" he asked.

"My husband. He would hunt me down. He would kill me." Ruby was crying now. Tears were rolling down her face. She reached for a tissue. She was feeling more helpless than when she walked through his door. Ruby hoped that she had made it very clear how she felt about taking this major step toward freedom.

"Call the police. They will help you get away. If he causes any problems, they will arrest him," the lawyer continued.

"No. Heavens no. I just couldn't do that. It would be just too humiliating," she replied with her eyes closed, shaking her head. She shuddered at the very thought of calling the police or even telling her doctor the secret of her dysfunctional marriage. "I'm so embarrassed that I have been subjected to the mental and physical abuse for so long and done nothing about it." She paused to catch her breath. "I have been told so often that all of this abuse was my fault. I just wasn't a good enough mother and wife. I honestly believe it must be my fault."

"Why do you continue to say no to my suggestions? You seem to be constantly putting roadblocks up. I understand that it will take a lot of guts to actually tell someone who can protect you about your situation. But these are not reasons to keep your secret."

"I know, but I'm so afraid of him."

"Ruby, just how long has this been going on?"

"I am so ashamed … for most of our married life, almost twenty-two years." She paused. "I'm not going to ever get away from him, am I?"

"Yes, you will. You just need to be very careful—actually, cautious. Gather documents. Take photos of your bruises. My advice is that you not let him know you're doing this. Also, you must tell someone about the danger you are faced with, like the police, your doctor, or a trusted male friend."

"Okay. I think I can do that." She wasn't sure, but she felt like this man had just given her more hope of freedom than she ever thought she was entitled to.

"Ruby, with these new facts you've just revealed, it's imperative that you positively make sure that you have everything legally documented to protect yourself. Photos of your injuries are best. You know what they say—a picture is worth a thousand words. Plus, it is difficult to deny physical evidence when you have a doctor's report and a photo. I also think it's time for you to confide in a friend or family member, just in case he gets more violent. I hope this doesn't happen, but he wouldn't be the first violent husband who followed through on his murderous threat."

"Oh," she sighed. "I don't know. I've been silent for so long. Won't people wonder why now?"

"No. Close friends can be good for you right now," he said, encouraging her to let her inner circle of friends into her secret world. "Make sure the friend or family member knows about his threat to kill you. Next time he starts to hit you, tell your husband that you have told someone about his threats."

"I don't think the police will do anything about a threat. At this point, it is my word against his," she argued. "I heard that one abused woman called the police but they only took her husband to the main sidewalk and talked to him."

"Then what happened?"

"The police left. He came back into the house and just continued the beating where he left off." She felt so small, almost invisible. "She ended up in hospital. She didn't even lay charges, as she was afraid he would find her and kill her."

"That's unfortunate. I'm sorry. But not all of these situations end like that. Be brave, Ruby."

"I appreciate your compassion and empathy. It was good to talk about my situation. Maybe the ice is cracked, and I'll be able to broach the topic with someone else."

Mr. Brown ended the one-hour free consultation with a supportive comment. "I'm here and would be pleased to handle the legal agreements and divorce. Please! You have to be very brave, as the situation may get worse. Keep in touch, and good luck to you."

Ruby stood and offered her hand. "Thank you, Mr. Brown, for your support and suggestions. I see that I have a tough road ahead of me before I'm free from more physical and mental abuse and threats. Thank you, and bye for now."

Without Ruby's knowledge, her lawyer, Eric, wrote a red alert note on her file. It read: *Ruby Monroe appears to be highly educated and a professional businesswoman. Unfortunately, the poor woman seems to be terribly ill-informed about her rights. Follow-up required—phone call end of this month for an update on her status.*

Ruby walked out of the lawyer's office with the nagging feeling she might not be better off with the lawyer's advice. She felt more frightened now than she had before she revealed her situation. At least, status quo, she knew how to deal with Jason, even though she remained his punching bag. She had to find the courage to take on the monster. She was reminded of fairy tales from her childhood. She had to be the one to slay the dragon to get her freedom. She would need to be strong—oh, so very strong.

This new information took up space in her head. She was preoccupied with her thoughts as she drove to her meeting with George. She couldn't wait until she was alone so she could spend quality time reviewing her situation and planning her exit from her marriage and the family home. She was confident that obtaining the documents would be fairly easy. A photo of her bruises would be a challenge. That was something she needed to work out.

Turning her thoughts to this evening's meeting, she put her personal issues on the back burner. *Compartmentalize, girl!*

She had been surprised at George's announcement that morning. She wasn't sure what this would mean to her. She knew full well that she'd secretly had a crush on him for some time. Maybe she just wanted to be with someone who made her feel good about herself.

She reviewed their previous work-related encounters. Yes, she had developed warm thoughts toward him. She acknowledged to herself that she did like him. He was a very interesting guy. He had a lot of accountability and responsibility in his position, and from all reports, he did his job well. He was popular and always fun to be around.

George was slightly over six feet tall, with a solid but not overweight body. She'd never describe him as having an athletic body—maybe cuddly like a big teddy bear. *Now that's a better description.* He was definitely a handsome guy, with little-boy puffy pink cheeks and a twinkle in his sky blue eyes. When George smiled, his whole face lit up, and his eyes sparkled.

He was a good manager. It was obvious that his staff liked him very much. She'd been told by several of his employees that they really enjoyed working for him.

She pulled into the almost vacant parking lot at Howard Johnsons and thought, *Good choice, George.* She was ten minutes late and hoped he didn't think she had stood him up. She entered the bar and instantly became aware of the speakers that wailed out large steel drum Caribbean music. That sound had always been one her very favourites. Even though she had never been to Jamaica, she enjoyed the music. A trip to the Caribbean and specifically Jamaica was on her bucket list.

Quickly she surveyed the lounge. Mostly she checked for familiar faces other than George's. Then her eyes settled on him. He sat at a small wooden table way back in the shadows of the dimly lit bar. He had already ordered a beer for himself and a glass of white wine for her.

When George spotted her walking toward his table, he smiled. "Thanks for meeting me again. I've been looking forward to this all day."

Ruby knew George cared about her—more than he was prepared to admit. When she reached his table, he stood and gave her a warm welcome with a bear hug. She sat on the chair he pulled out with an exaggerated bowing gesture for her to join him. She accepted his offer and graciously sat. She acknowledged his playful invitation, smiled and said, "Thank you, George. Such a gentleman you are. Sorry I'm a little late. I had an errand to run first."

They casually chatted about work and superficial subjects that gave them time to get accustomed to each other's company outside of the office. It also gave George the time he needed to review exactly how he wanted to say what was in his head.

There were a few awkward quiet moments while they sipped their drinks and surveyed the lounge. Then George looked directly at her and started to cry. Tears ran down his flushed cheeks. His shoulders were hunched over, indicating how humbled and hurt he was feeling. It was obvious to Ruby that his heart was broken.

He blurted out, "Ruby, my wife has left me for a guy at her work." Through his blubbering and mumbles, she was enlightened. "Our marriage was already on the rocks," he said. "I don't really know just which incident lately made me suspicious, but her recent behaviour has been questionable. We have become estranged. I don't think we have had much to say to each other lately. I must admit that the divorce discussion this weekend wasn't a complete shock to me, but it still hurt," he continued between sobs. "I feel violated and betrayed."

She reached into her purse and handed him a tissue. She watched while he wiped away his tears and blew his nose. Ruby all of a sudden felt very deep compassion for him. She so wanted to go to him, hug and comfort him, but they didn't have a personal relationship, only an open friendly business one, and therefore it was "hands off." Plus, this was neither the time nor the place for that kind of a blatant display of affection, even if they wanted it.

"What can I do to help?" she asked.

"It's my daughter, Tammy. She's just 3 years old. That's such an impressionable age. I love her so much. I can't lose her. I just can't," he cried. He continued to confide in her. "Ruby, what am I going to do?"

"I'm so sorry that this is happening to you."

"More important, I'm so afraid that she might forget me. I really do love that sweet little girl. You know, the father–daughter connection is definitely there for us. She cried and reached out for me when my wife tore her away from me and then bolted out of the house on Saturday. Tammy knew something was wrong. How do you explain this stuff to a 3-year-old?"

"I don't know," she said, trying to console him. She knew he didn't know that she had her troubles too. "I'm sure it isn't hard for a father who's been faithful to get visitation rights." She tried her best to take the high road when comforting him.

The back-and-forth conversation that went on for another hour was full of ideas, suggestions and what-ifs. "I'm sorry to unload on you like that," he said finally. "I just had to talk to someone who I could trust and know they wouldn't blab it all around the office." He attempted to gain his composure and lighten up the conversation. Faking half a smile, he said, "So how was your day?"

"Not much better than yours." She lowered her eyes and coyly smiled.

Ruby in her wildest dreams would never have guessed that they would end up commiserating with each other. But she had to talk to someone. "The reason I was a little late for this meeting with you was, I took advantage of a free first consultation with a lawyer in town," she said. She was determined to hold back the details of her conversation with the lawyer, at least for now. George had enough on his own plate.

"C'mon. You can't do that. You're making me feel guilty about dumping my problems on you. I'm a good listener too," he said, encouraging her to share more details.

"I believe that you are, and I do trust you. I feel kind of strange saying this because we do not, or at least *did not,* have that kind of relationship before tonight. But here it is. I'm filing for divorce. Welcome to the club." She grinned with satisfaction, as this was the first time she had actually said it out loud. She secretly hoped he was interested enough in her as a person to eventually let her tell her story. But she couldn't unload the horrible details of her useless private life right now. She was sure those details would scare him away.

Being here with George was like an escape from reality for her. Being a male, he probably would take Jason's side anyway. *Men all stick together, right?*

After all, she had become convinced that she probably deserved everything that Jason did to her; he had told her that enough times. On some level, she had started to believe him. She knew she desperately needed a trusted friend who she could talk to, but a female friend would be easier for her to share her pitiful life with. She was afraid to share too many details. There was just too much at stake. The specifics were way too embarrassing and humiliating.

Listen to me, she thought. *I'm not ready to share with anyone. I hadn't realized how pathetic I must sound. I'm definitely not ready for that conversation.*

George reached across the table and put his hand on top of hers. "Please," he said. "I can see you're hurting. Tell me, please."

"I think I'll need another glass of wine to build up the courage to share those details with you or anyone else." *I'm not sure if even then I would be able to tell him how unbearable my home life has been for so many years.*

They ordered another round. While waiting for the drinks to arrive, they chatted about people at work—mostly gossip. The thought immediately came to Ruby's mind: *who's bedding down who or whom.*

He asked, "Did you know our fearless leader and president is screwing the new sales rep, Jennifer?"

"Gee, and he's so charming," she said with a sarcastic sneer. Then, with the help of the wine she had just consumed, she added, "Last Christmas when he made the rounds to wish everyone happy holidays, he cornered me in my office. The dirty old man's Christmas kiss was a tongue right down my throat. I thought I would throw up or at the very least choke. How do you tell the president to 'Fuck off' and still keep your job? You just don't," she said, pulling a face and waving the thought off with her hand.

"Unfortunately," she continued, "he depended on that. He has the power. This is the environment we—meaning women—are forced to work in. My experience is that the cosmetics business is full of these creeps with egos the size of battleships. Whoa, I had better stop there, as I've already said way more than I originally intended."

"Does the president always kiss the female employees at Christmas?" asked George.

"No, not traditionally. Just a dirty old man looking for some nookie or to shock."

She was worried that George probably had a lower impression of her by now. She caught herself and stopped, because she knew better, but somehow she didn't believe that she would ever be thought of as the victim. That was a new concept for her.

Regardless, she could not tell him about the personal hell she had lived in for so many years. She had never even hinted, never mind outright told anyone—friends or family—about the nightmare she lived every single day. One might describe her as a mentally wounded soldier. They called it post-traumatic stress syndrome. As a result of being a victim of her twenty years of war, aka marriage, she guessed she could be diagnosed with PTSD.

Ruby internally agonized over the decision to share her story. She didn't know how to tell someone that she was the victim of an abusive man. How embarrassing it would be to actually say that out loud. *Just how do you say, "My husband frequently beats me and is also an adulterer?"* Wow, that would be so humiliating. No, I could never tell him. He would think that I must be the most miserable person on earth to live with. How do you tell someone and keep his respect? How?

Another round of drinks arrived. They casually sipped and chatted some more, and then finally he asked, "Well, are you going to share your story with me? I promise not to judge."

Looking across the table at George, she hesitated for a moment to mull over in her mind the answer to that question. She so wanted to believe that she could trust him with her very private secret. But you don't change in just a few minutes and start to trust again. No, it would take more time. Lots more time. It had taken twenty years to get to this place in hell, and a couple of drinks and supportive chatter would not change many, many years of fear and distrust. Through repeated betrayal, her perception was that there were always consequences of trusting. Thanks to Jason, Ruby had learned nothing good ever came of trusting a partner. Like it or not, this was her proven experience.

After a longish pause, Ruby finally responded, "Sorry, not this time. You have enough on your plate." She wondered, *Have I been brainwashed by Jason? Is he doing this just to keep me in the marriage?* This may not have been a correct assumption, but it was what she got out of the meeting with the lawyer and how she felt.

Eventually, they exhausted the workplace gossip. Ruby said, "I really need to get home, as I don't want to get caught in a lie to my husband. I told Jason that I'm interviewing some applicants for a vacant position. This wouldn't cause him to be suspicious. Evening appointments are necessary for this job, because not everyone is able to attend employment interviews during business hours. So my lie is plausible."

They walked to their cars. She said, "Good night, George. Sorry it was such a sad evening for you. Regardless, I enjoyed your company. Thanks."

His eyes twinkled as he smiled and said, "Good night. Maybe we can get together again?" It was more of a question than a statement.

Silence surrounded them along with many unanswered questions. Secrecy about her constant abuse was a heavy load for her to carry; she had to put on a brave front for George, family and siblings. She couldn't tell any of them because she assumed they, especially George, would think of her as foolish, stupid, or maybe even spineless.

Deep in thought, she drove home. During the drive, she wondered: *Where is this all going? Is it going anywhere?*

Chapter 22

1978: Another Problem

Ruby had just finished the family laundry when she got an unwanted surprise. She'd folded Jason's clean underwear and socks as usual. While in the process of putting them away in his dresser, she was taken aback when she noticed a small brown prescription bottle. She reached for it and read the label. *What is this?* She had never seen this prescription and didn't even know Jason had a prescription. She was even more surprised that it was prescribed for the treatment of herpes. *What's herpes? Is it a sexually transmitted disease?* She knew deep down that his promiscuous sexual activity would eventually catch up to him.

She checked her medical dictionary at home and then searched the medical books at the local library. Her mouth dropped when she learned it was a highly contagious disease. The medical dictionary described it as commonly transmitted during sexual contact. Her heart dropped into her stomach. Jason had never mentioned anything to her about this, nor did he ever use a condom when they had sex. It was bad enough that he apparently had unprotected sex with his other female partners. She couldn't get her mind around why he didn't use a condom with her or tell her he was being treated for herpes. That was just fundamentally mean and inconsiderate.

Jason used to say he liked rough sex. She did not like to be pushed and shoved around during foreplay. In her mind, he was just plain crude. Maybe the other women he had sex with liked it rough; in reality, it was rape. No wonder she'd lost interest in him as a sexual partner. His advances did nothing for her. During this dry spell, he frequently got frustrated with her lack of interest and so he forced himself on her. Of course, he never ever wore protection.

Worried and unsure what herpes meant to her, she needed to pursue other avenues. Confident the best way to get accurate information about herpes would be their family physician, she made an appointment.

Following her complete body and mouth exam, her doctor took a vaginal and an oral swab. She asked, "Why my mouth?"

The doctor asked, "Have you ever performed oral sex on your husband?"

"Yes. Damn him, yes."

"Ruby, you seem to have several bruises. How did you get them?"

"Oh, I'm kind of clumsy, always walking into something. I'm okay." She gathered her clothes, dressed and left the doctor's office, almost wishing she hadn't come. It didn't take a genius to see the doctor was not satisfied with her answer about the bruises. More humiliation. When would it end?

When she got home, she plopped down on the couch and sat there in a daze. She allowed her tears to escape. *He just keeps doing it to me, doesn't he?* she sobbed.

The doctor's office phoned a couple of days later. "Hello, Mrs. Munroe?"

"Yes," Ruby said cautiously, fearing bad news. She had tried hard to not feel depressed about this latest calamity. Ruby felt like she was being pushed over the edge of an abyss. She had been crying a lot lately and wondered if his cruelty and adulterous behaviour had finally brought her to a breaking point.

"It's Betsy, the receptionist at Doctor Martin's office. I have good news for you. Your tests came back, and I'm happy to tell you you're clear."

"Thank you! That really *is* good news, Betsy." Fortunately, she didn't have herpes. This *was* the best news.

Nevertheless, the herpes incident was the proverbial last straw. She knew she must be stronger than ever. She had to make positive plans. In fact, she wrote up a timeline, just so she would know that her exit was on schedule.

Again she met with her attorney. He called it follow-up and didn't charge her. Ruby understood that she was a case he was keeping pretty close tabs on. Also, she had told him she didn't have much money of her own. She, like a good wife and at Jason's insistence, had always put all of her money into the family pot. Well, not always. She was determined to not let this little hurdle deter her, not this time. Jason didn't know that when she got a raise, overtime, or bonus money, she deposited it in her secret bank account.

The first snowfall was delightful. Children made snowballs the size of tennis balls for their annual snowball fight. It was now officially winter, regardless of what the calendar said.

For Ruby, winter meant something different this year. Her plan, according to her schedule, was to leave Jason and have a fresh start with the New Year. Enough was enough. In her mind, she'd already had way too much to deal with in her young life. He had stolen her youth. He had made her life a living hell. She was older now, and hopefully, she was also wiser. She definitely earned good money and was convinced that she could support herself. She deposited her latest raise into her secret bank account, aka her escape fund.

Ruby knew she was strong and a fighter. She was determined to succeed. *Be brave,* she told herself, *or suffer another year of abuse and the pain of loneliness. Which is it going to be? Come on, make up your mind. You must be strong and determined.*

When Jason finally woke on this particular Saturday morning, he sauntered into the kitchen for his usual massive weekend breakfast of bacon, eggs, toast and fried leftover spaghetti—all prepared and served to him, the man of the house, by Ruby. His appreciation was shown with little more than a grunt; definitely not "thanks." This was her job, and she was expected to make him breakfast. After all, he was the main breadwinner. Of course, she also brought in a healthy amount of money as well. She handed over her whole paycheque, which wasn't too shabby, just like she was expected to. This she had come to regret.

Finally, she was committed and determined to follow her plan. She was suffocating. She didn't like the feeling of being trapped in this marriage. Her life was an absolute nightmare. She carefully read their large weekend newspaper but spent most of her time perusing the classified ads, looking for rental apartments that she could afford.

No more procrastinating. She knew what she had to do. No time like the present. She took a deep breath, closed her eyes, mustered up more courage and then blurted out, "Jason, I'm leaving, and I want a divorce."

"Yeah, and what are you going to live on? You're going nowhere," he snarled as he turned his attention back to the sports section.

"I *am* really going to leave you this time. I have had it. Enough is enough." She stood firm in her conviction, on the outside. Internally, her stomach was doing summersaults.

Once again, he glared at her and then raised himself from his chair. With his hands firmly planted on his hips in his most intimidating stance, he spat,

"Use your head, stupid. You know I will kill you if you ever try to leave. At the very least ruin you, so no one else will ever want you."

Ruby was adamant. She had decided she would rather die than live any longer with the monster she married.

"I don't care anymore. You don't frighten me. I'm leaving you," she stated with the strongest commitment and bravest posture she could present. Inside she trembled with fear. *I think I'm going to throw up.* Ruby ran to the powder room with her hand tightly clasped over her mouth.

"Sure, now you're being smart." Jason took her sudden exodus from the kitchen as a sign that she had decided to not pursue the divorce threat.

What was she doing? He had promised to kill her on several occasions when she told him that she wanted to divorce him. Each and every time, he threatened to kill her and the kids. Previously, she had backed down, as she thought that she just couldn't let that happen. She always believed she needed to find another way out of this hell. Not this time. Her determination did not waver. She was leaving. Death would be better than the cruelty she had endured for so many years now. She called his bluff.

About ten minutes later, Ruby returned to the kitchen. She stood with firmly planted feet and stated, "This time I will not back down. No, Jason, I *am* leaving."

"I will kill you. Trust me."

Ruby left his threat of doing her harm hanging in the air.

Why would anyone with half a brain allow such abuse to happen to them, and for so long? She could hear them in her head. She knew these labels might currently describe her, but deep down none of them defined her.

She had become withdrawn. Never again would she be able to share intimate feelings. Jason had taught her that her inner feelings and fears would always be used against her. He deprived her of ever having an open friendship with anyone due to his betrayal and badgering. This destroyed many aspects of her life and interfered with or affected every relationship thereafter.

Chapter 23

1978: Married Twenty-Two Years

A few weeks later, once again, she was on her way to meet George for a drink. She smiled. It was good to feel happy. She had forgotten what it felt like to feel so cheerful. She didn't like lying to Jason, but it was simpler than the truth. By now, she wasn't really certain what the truth was or how deep her developing feelings were for George right now. She did like him. At the thought of seeing him again, she got those old familiar twinges. They caused her to fidget in her car seat. By now she was well aware of what horny felt like. She *was* horny.

George had called her into his office earlier that day and asked if she would meet him this evening, same place and same time. When she drove into the parking lot of the now familiar Howard Johnson's, she was excited but cautious. She wondered, *What am I doing here?*

Ruby visualized George's infectious smile. She felt like his curly dark brown hair was begging her to run her fingers through it. She had heard around the office that George was somewhat of a party boy. Boy? Yes. After all, he was ten years younger than her. It was easy for her to check his age, as she had access to his personnel file. She also noticed that his marital status had been recently changed to "separated."

They both broke into broad smiles when she arrived at the booth. She slid across the bench seat and made herself comfortable. The dim romantic lighting hid a multitude of sins in this older worn-out lounge. She decided that she probably wouldn't stay if the bright lights were on and actually showed the soiled carpet beneath her feet.

He flashed his beautiful welcoming smile and moved a glass closer to Ruby. "Here. I assumed white wine for you?"

"Yes. Thank you."

"No, thank *you* for accepting another invitation, I really wanted to see you again."

Coyly, Ruby agreed. "Me too."

"Are you okay?"

"Yes. I am now. Seeing you is the high point of my day."

"What, if anything, have you done about your divorce?"

"I'm embarrassed to say nothing. That doesn't mean that I won't."

She knew he had an agenda, even though he kept his motivation to himself. Ruby read people for a living. It didn't take a genius to interpret his goal. She also noted that George would not be a good poker player. He blushed far too easily.

Ruby felt the sexual tension between them. She became aroused at the very suggestion of having sex, which she anticipated would be wild and explosive. *Careful, Ruby. Don't get taken in. It's far too soon*, she told herself. *I must change the subject to something safer.*

She returned his welcoming smile and then cautiously asked, "How are things going with Tammy? Is she adjusting okay? I assume you found a nice place to stay?"

"Yes, but I've been very lonely. I don't like these arrangements at all. I do have visitation every other weekend and alternate Wednesday evenings. To be honest, that's really not good enough, but it's way better than no visitation rights at all," he added.

She saw that his face captured the immensity of his pain.

"I know this really is shared custody, but I want more," he added.

"You can probably renegotiate, as you both are working parents, and you said your wife works out of town several days each month."

"But why am I being punished when it was *her* who had the affair, not me? I was always faithful to her. Sure, I joke around, but that's all it ever was—just innocent flirting."

"George, sometimes life just isn't fair," Ruby responded. He couldn't know that her comment was based on deep-seated feelings founded on her own life experiences.

"I did rent an apartment down near the lake," he enthusiastically shared, displaying a playful smile. "I don't have too much furniture yet, though. I need to buy more stuff—at least a sofa bed or something along that line." He hesitated and looked down at the table as if he was planning the rest of his sentence. "My ex told me last weekend that she will not let Tammy continue to stay over if the next time she brings her over there isn't a better place for her to sleep. Right now, the only place is on the mattress—my bed. She was quite emphatic that Tammy can't sleep with me, her dad. She says that it's just too creepy."

Then he coyly smiled. "Would you like to see my place?" he asked with a definite twinkle in his eye.

Ruby thought, *This is the perfect time to ask the big question—or, some might say, deal with the elephant in the room.* "George, do you know how old I am?"

"No, and I don't care. You're a great gal, and I like you a lot. You might not like what I'm about to say, so I'll preface it by telling you I mean it with the utmost respect and admiration. Please accept it as a compliment. You have a maturity level that I'm not used to. Women my age and younger are so giddy, superficial and always flaunting their sexuality, as if that is a good basis to start a relationship. Maybe a one-night stand, but certainly not a relationship. I do not want a continuous string of one-night stands. I want a real relationship that will last for a while. That quickie, 'let's jump into the sack,' one-night-stand mindset is a turnoff for me. You, on the other hand, are a very sexy person. For me, you ooze sexuality from every pore," he said, pleading his case.

Ruby thought, *George, you have no idea what I would like for you or me in bed. You really turn me on. I would so love to show you how I make love.*

"Thank you," she said. "Those comments make me feel good about myself. That isn't something I have experienced very often, especially these days. My self-esteem is low these days. I don't want to mislead you, but I do want to set the record straight. I am a full ten years older than you." It was important to Ruby that she make sure she wasn't misrepresenting herself in any way. She knew that it was rare at this time for women to be involved with a younger man with this big of an age gap. She let this information settle before speaking again. "I hope that I'm not assuming something that was not in your invitation to see your apartment."

"Made. I admit it," he said and coyly grinned.

It was her turn to bashfully smile and nod her head in the affirmative.

"I did have exactly that specific idea in mind," he added. "I'm definitely physically attracted to you."

I can't let you know how much we agree on in that department. Ruby was inwardly fighting to resist him and avoid making a big mistake.

"Your age is immaterial to me," he went on. "I just thought, if you're alone and I'm alone, why not spend time together?" he said with that familiar sparkle in his eye and a big wide grin that displayed as much sincerity as he could muster.

"George, I'm flattered, but I'm not free to see anyone. I need to take care of my personal business first. I don't want to ever be accused of leaving Jason for you. I want to leave Jason for me. This is very important for me. I need to get out of my marriage first. I do not want any distractions, like you. I'm afraid that if we entered into a sexual relationship, feelings would just get muddled. If that happened, it wouldn't work out for either one of us. I think I would feel like I was settling for something that I was not actually free to have."

She continued, "If you're still available when I'm legally free, then we can do whatever we want, but let's not spoil our friendship with the one-night-stand passion and sex thing. I want something more for us. Most importantly, I also want a life without abuse."

One thing Ruby had learned from her little sexual fling with Ron Battle was that she wanted more, especially from George.

"See, that's what I'm talking about," he said. "Maturity and sincerity, all in one beautiful package."

She so wanted to be with him, to feel his hot breath on her face, neck and breasts. Her nipples were hardening just thinking about him licking them. Oh, she was feeling so very, very horny right now. She yearned for him to gently fondle and caress her aching aroused body with his beautiful soft hands. *Stop! Get a hold of yourself, girl.* Right now, she knew that she must put those thoughts in the back of her mind for another time. She did not want or need this complication right now.

They talked for another hour, and then they walked out of their favourite meeting place together. When they stopped at their cars to say good night, he reached over and gathered her into his strong muscular arms and gave her the most deliciously satisfying hug she had ever experienced. "Ruby I don't know what you have been through, but I can tell you that I would never treat you badly. I promise."

That was it. Now she had the strength and motivation to proceed with the divorce. She really wanted to be with George, but she had to put her plans into action and clean up her situation first.

Chapter 24

1978 – Late Summer

Ruby was now totally committed to her plan. The first step of her strategy was to each week take ten dollars from her allotted grocery money and put it safely away in a newly opened bank account in her name only. Unfortunately, Jason caught on to that plan too quickly.

Next, she shopped with the plan to return approximately ten dollars of her grocery purchases each week and keep the refund. She also offered to do chores for their neighbours, like watching their children in the evening or if they had an appointment during the day on the weekend and needed a sitter. This plan worked. She earned good money and put every cent into her new personal and secret bank account at a different bank than the one they used as a family. She was physically exhausted, but finally, she succeeded in outsmarting him.

By mid-December, she had stashed away—counting her raises, bonuses and other sources—nearly two thousand dollars for a deposit on an apartment. Now, with the desire to leave on her timetable, she scoured the rental ads every day looking for leases that she could afford and were in good areas of the city. Once she left, she would be able to keep all of her salary. That thought alone gave her a mental boost. Based on her calculation, she chose three apartments in her price range and in an area close enough to work but not too close.

Ruby made appointments with the superintendents of each building for the following Tuesday right after work. She carefully inspected each rental, looking for well-kept buildings with amenities, as there was no room in her budget for a fitness club.

She was successful and very pleased with herself. Ruby was delighted with the third apartment she viewed. The building was clean and freshly painted. The layout of the rooms appealed to her decor logic. The kitchen appeared to be old but scrubbed clean. This apartment also had an extra bedroom should Matt or Joey decide to visit and stay over. Ruby gave the superintendent a cheque for both first and last month's rent. With her hand shaking from excitement, she signed the lease.

She drove home giddy with anticipation of her new home. After twenty-plus years, she was finally going to be free. She didn't know how she was going to be able to contain her ecstatic mood once she got home. Then she remembered she had to compartmentalize, and that is how she hoped to keep her secret from Jason.

Gradually, without causing too much attention, whenever she was home alone, she started to pack cartons on the sly. She hid packed boxes under beds, in closets under clothes and beneath stuff stored in the garage. Due to necessity, she had to be very creative.

Unfortunately, Jason got suspicious. A week before Christmas, he confronted her. "What are you doing?" he asked, grabbing her arm tightly. "I've noticed some changes and things in different places. Why do you think that's happening?" He didn't want to hear her lie or tell him a story; he was pretty sure he already knew. "You're packing because your moving, aren't you?"

"Look, I don't want any trouble, please," she responded in a quiet monotone voice. The last thing she wanted was to set him into one of his rages.

"I noticed there's a weird calmness about you and a willingness to jump to my every demand. Let me remind you, I will *not* let you go. You are *not* leaving me. I promise. I will kill you if you ever try to leave me."

"Jason, I cannot continue to live here with your abuse. I'm afraid to say or do anything for fear of setting you off on one of your rampages. I would leave for my own sanity." She was outwardly still calm, but inside she felt her stomach twist. She was resigned to the possible outcome. Her death was not an unwelcome solution. It was not the one she wanted, but she had to challenge him. Call his bluff.

As expected, Jason did not disappoint. He flew into a rage, and a huge physical and verbal fight ensued. She heard all about the things he had done for her in his mind.

He shouted at her, "You're an ungrateful useless bitch. How could you do this to your children? You're abandoning them, and me. Don't you care anymore? Who are you screwing? You must be seeing someone. I'll have you followed. You won't get a cent from me."

Interesting he accuses me of indiscretions. He's the adulterer. Well, I guess that's not totally true anymore.

Ruby tried to ignore him. She calmly said, "Jason, I'm not leaving because of anyone except you." *Maybe he's bluffing, I don't know, but I am certain that I will not be deterred in my quest for freedom.*

He said, "Ha, ha, I knew you were getting ready to leave. If you know what's good for you and your darling children, you'd be wise to reconsider your plans."

Ruby gathered her courage and, for the first time, stood her ground. She decided that she would no longer be intimidated by him. "Enough is enough. I will not be your personal punching bag any longer." She was firm and didn't back down this time. She used the advice that the lawyer had given her. She lied by telling him, "I have warned my boss, Mr. Wilson, that if I do not come to work, he should notify the police, as that will mean my husband has murdered me."

Jason momentarily stopped in his tracks, but not for long. He proceeded to shove her down eight stairs to the landing. She felt each step as it met with her shoulder, hips and head. On the landing, she appeared once again to be a pile of clothing waiting to be laundered, just lying there in a clump. She was bruised and hurt. His actions reinforced her need to leave. Nothing he did to her now would deter her. In fact, she was more dedicated than ever to her plan.

Actually, his actions just made her stronger-willed and more adamant. This time she was *really* leaving. She wanted to do the right thing, for her, for the first time in her married life.

The next morning, he changed his tactic. He decided to beg. He pleaded, "Please stay at least until Christmas is over. Think of the kids. What kind of Christmas will it be for them if you aren't here? Ruby, don't be selfish. Think of someone other than yourself for a change."

Ruby watched him carefully. *What's he up to now? Is this his new game?* Ruby had to always be on guard when he swiftly changed his approach. She didn't trust him.

Jason said, "As usual, we've already invited my mom and dad for Christmas dinner, plus two of my brothers and their wives. Please don't spoil my parents' Christmas too. Let's keep this as our little secret for now, shall we?"

I get it! He doesn't want anyone to know that I'm planning on leaving him or why.

"You know I love your parents very much. I wouldn't do anything to make them unhappy. Okay, I'll stay, but only until Christmas is past," she said, reluctantly agreeing to postpone her move out.

She had always wondered if he was so ashamed of his behaviour it would be easier for him if she was dead and couldn't tell anyone.

He asked, "Why spoil everyone else's Christmas just because you're being so selfish?"

There's the real Jason. His true colors are showing again. She was determined to not be fazed by this complete about-face attitude. Once she agreed to stay, he turned nasty. She could have predicted this without a crystal ball. What he didn't know was that she had rented an apartment starting January first. She couldn't leave until January anyway. But she'd let him beg. It looked good on him. She felt like she had gained strength and there was a strong wind at her back pushing her in the right direction—away from him.

She knew he realized that he wouldn't be able to talk her out of leaving or plead with her not to throw away their twenty-two years of marriage. *Throw it away? Who is he kidding? Nothing, except the children, about this marriage is worth keeping.* Watching him change, she realized that he had come to terms with the truth: brutality wasn't going to win this battle of wills.

He said, "Look, I'm trying to be the rational person here. I will not try to stop you from moving in January if you agree to stay here over the holidays."

But he had lied so often before, she just didn't believe him anymore. She would be a fool to fall for his game. She reconsidered only because he did have a point: why spoil Christmas for everyone else, including mom and dad Monroe and Jason's brothers and sisters-in-law. They, to her knowledge, knew nothing about the abuse she had suffered. If she spoiled the holidays, then she felt like she would become the bad person. If she stayed, her secret was safe.

"Okay. I'll agree to stay." She hoped this would stop his verbal and physical attacks on her. What he still didn't know, and she would not tell him, was that she had to stay until New Year's Day. She had nowhere to go until then. His lack of this knowledge had given her a bargaining chip she hadn't realized she had. She could actually openly pack boxes now. *One for Ruby!* She secretly congratulated herself with a glass of wine.

The week after Christmas was a week from hell, with constant bullying, pushing and shoving. His attitude got uglier by the day. He forced her to have unprotected sex several times, even though he still had herpes. He raped her again and again almost daily for the whole week. Her vagina was raw from the lack of lubrication and the rough penetration. He didn't even bother to call it making love anymore.

They constantly fought over the least little issue. For the first time, she saw his desperation and vulnerability.

She prayed she could survive just one more week. She could not wait to get out of this house and away from him forever. She tolerated his abusive behaviour. She became submissive and didn't fight back. He became less abusive, as if he knew he had won or lost the battle.

Chapter 25

1979: Moving Day

She had secretly booked a moving van for Monday, January 6, at 9:00 a.m. She knew he would leave for work long before that time. He didn't know when she was actually planning to move out. It was possible he'd convinced himself that he had intimidated her enough, and she would be too afraid of his threats and therefore too fearful to move out.

She had previously gathered Matt and Joey together for a secret meeting. She swore them to secrecy and explained her need to move out before something terrible happened. Ruby pledged her love to them and offered to take them with her to her new home. The boys, disgusted with their father's behaviour, had moved out of the house long before.

The Friday afternoon just before her planned move, Ruby was on her way to a meeting with the manager of accounting when she saw George walking toward her in a secluded corridor that ran next to his office. She grinned when she announced, "I've rented an apartment and booked the moving van. I'm moving out this coming Monday morning. My emotions are running the whole gamut. I'm ecstatic, hesitant, nervous and frightened that Jason will try to stop me." She paused long enough to catch her breath and then continued, "If all goes as planned, I will be arriving at my new place just before noon on Monday. I just so want to be free of him."

"Slow down," he said as he smiled back at her with that oh-so-familiar twinkle in his gorgeous blue eyes. He could see the happiness and relief in both her eyes and her face. He was pleased for her and said, "Ruby, that's great news. I know this is a major step for you. Let me know if you need any help. I'm here for you. What's your new address?"

"150 Grayson Drive, apartment 506."

George cautioned her, "Please be very careful and *please* call the police at the first sign of trouble. Do *not* wait. Maybe if he hears that the police are responding, he'll back off."

Ruby's heart skipped a beat when she saw the moving van pull into the driveway. She worried, *What if Jason plans to return home and catch me in the act of moving? My stomach's in knots. My chest is tight. I can't breathe. Pull yourself together, girl. You can have a panic attack later.*

With hurried commands, she instructed the movers, "Load the dining room and living room furniture and the master bedroom suite first."

"Ms. Monroe, are there cartons and clothing?" the movers asked.

"Of course, but load all of the packed cartons after the furniture. There's nothing breakable in the cartons—just linens, towels and kitchen necessities. But I want everything out of the house first, please."

Everything was brought to the driveway and loaded into the van. Ruby gave orders like a drill sergeant. Panic will do that to the best-laid plans.

When the truck was packed and only then did she divulge the address of her new home. Relieved and elated that she had succeeded in the first lap of the move, she drove the car that she had been relegated to drive—a small four-cylinder gray Pinto—to her new home. Jason drove the big newer Country Squire station wagon. It just didn't matter, because she was finally going to be free of him.

Meanwhile, at 150 Grayson Drive, Ruby's new apartment building, George was waiting impatiently. He paced back and forth in the lobby, worried that Ruby's husband would try to stop her from finally being free. George checked his image reflected in the mirrored wall. Since his separation, he had lost at least twenty pounds. Now his six-foot frame was more slender, and his clothes fit way better. This pleased him, as he thought he looked healthier. Also, his cheeks were less chubby without those extra pounds. He hoped Ruby would agree with his self-assessment. A closer look at his hair convinced him that he had a few more gray hairs interspersed in his full head of curly dark brown locks. He was sure it was mostly due to the stress of his separation.

Ruby arrived just before the moving van. He watched her confidently walk across the parking lot toward the lobby. He had worried for her safety. He was afraid that her husband would follow through with his threats to do her harm. Shaking his head, he realized he couldn't even say the words—kill her. George had a soft spot for a professional well-put-together woman, especially Ruby. He still found her very attractive. Most of all, he loved her smile. He liked that her whole face always lit up whenever she saw him.

He greeted her with a smile, a big warm bear hug and a bouquet of flowers. George's, smiling face shouted his happiness at seeing her. "Here, welcome to your new home," he said, bowing while handing her the colourful spray of flowers. "Handyman George, at your beck and call. I'm here to help you settle into your new place. I hope you don't mind," he added with his most charming smile.

Ruby hugged him back and said, "Thank you, George. You are so thoughtful." She smiled to herself and thought, *I don't even know if I brought a vase with me.* She mentally shook herself, because that didn't matter. She was finally free. "Your offer of assistance is perfect and very much appreciated. I know I can find something for you to do," she added with a playful smile and a come-on twinkle in her eyes.

Yes, George, I know what I would like to do with you. Just thinking about finally being able to be with him made her tingle in the most delicious way.

George and Ruby worked very hard for several hours placing the furniture around the apartment as the movers carried the pieces in from the truck. They unpacked several cartons she'd secretly filled with household items she wanted to bring with her and had stored in the garage until today. Ruby had brought sufficient necessities to make her kitchen and bathroom functional.

"George, would you please make the bed while I put the dishes in the cupboard? I think I'll feel more settled with fewer boxes stacked against the wall." She knew that she must keep her mind on unpacking for a little while longer. It was getting harder and harder to ignore her desire to tackle him in the bedroom. What a great opportunity. *No, wait. It will be perfect.* She just knew.

When they had finally finished putting everything in place, they were exhausted from the physical labour. Ruby suggested, "I think we should have something to eat." Unfortunately, the one thing she hadn't brought was food. She thought about going food shopping.

"Let me go to the mall across the street and pick up some takeout food." George gave her a sweet little peck on the cheek and then hurried off to find food.

Ruby raised her hand and touched her cheek, remembering the kiss.

Out of Silence

"George, hurry back, please." She had plans for him this evening. She really hoped that he had the same plans for her. It would be so nice to actually make love with someone she wanted to be with. No more unwanted brutal forced sex for her.

When he returned, he was grinning from ear to ear. He held up his right hand, which held a liquor store bag, and said, "Look what I found." His left hand held a fast-food paper bag containing burgers and fries. He placed the food on the table. Then, ceremoniously, with a bow and a wave of his hand across his chest, in a form that most butlers would be proud of, he removed the bottle of wine from the bag that was in his other raised hand. He found a corkscrew, which he used to open the wine. He searched until he found a couple of wineglasses, poured the wine and then offered Ruby a glass.

They ate their burgers and fries, chatting while eating and drinking as if they were old comfortable friends. With help of the wine, the mood turned electric, with vibes being sent with shy but sensual looks. Their tingling longing for each other's bodies was kept in check, as the anticipation was mixed with the unknown. This would be their first sexual encounter. It was as frightening as it was anticipated. Neither one knew what to expect from the other. She had wished for this day and fantasized how he would react. *I hope George wants me as much as I want him.* Neither one had any idea of what the reality of their encounter would be.

The conversation was filled with innuendo and suggestive comments. They flirted and gently touched when passing by or handing the other a replenished glass of wine. This playful behaviour helped break down the barriers that had been erected over the past months. Ruby was ready to play out her dreams of how this intimate moment would culminate. *I hope George is using the same playbook as me. If not, I think I might just explode.*

The only calmness in the room was the carefully chosen soft music on the stereo. They so enjoyed their picnic that evening and each other's company.

Ruby giggled like a schoolgirl in anticipation of what she hoped would come. The wine helped her ever-increasing horny mood. She was so happy to be with George in her new home. She was so very relaxed and aroused at the same time—never forgetting she was free at last.

They didn't know if it was the sense of joy or freedom, but the long-suppressed feelings exploded. Maybe it was the wine, or perhaps the sexual attraction and desire were always there. They didn't know or care. The atmosphere around them was charged. They both felt it.

It started with a little teasing, then flirting, which developed into gentle play slapping. It was like this frisky behaviour ignited the flame that had been smoldering just below the surface all day long.

Ruby coyly suggested, with an obvious grin that revealed her motivation, "I should have a shower to remove the grime and sweat from today's physical labour. Lugging boxes and moving furniture around all day only made it worse." She walked toward the bathroom. Looking back over her shoulder, she pinched her nose with two fingers to reinforce her statement that she thought she smelled bad.

George smiled in agreement. Ruby had no doubt about his desire to finally make mad passionate love to her. She watched as he wiggled and adjusted himself, making room in his pants for his much-enlarged penis, which she was looking forward to enjoying.

With highly aroused sexual feelings, Ruby hurried to the bathroom and stripped down. She dropped the soiled clothes from her tingling body in a pile in the middle of the bathroom floor. Stepping into the very warm invigorating shower, she was amazed at how sensuous the jets of water felt on her aroused breasts. Everything around her was sensual. *Wow! I'm so horny. I need to fuck him soon—very soon. I am going to come on my own if I wait very much longer.*

Standing there in the shower with her eyes closed and her imagination in high gear, she enjoyed the feeling of the warm water washing over her aroused body. Her thoughts were interrupted by the sound of the shower curtain being slowly pulled back, exposing George and his beautiful engorged penis as he entered the shower.

"Oh! How wonderful! Please join me," she said, smiling with the imagined pleasure that this wonderful member would provide. Ruby turned her face up to him and tilted her head back to look into his handsome face. She was searching for and then accepted his delicious tongue into her welcoming mouth.

He took her face in his hands and kissed her forehead, cheeks and finally her mouth ever so gently, then her eyelids and back to her hungry waiting mouth and tongue. Ruby sensually ran her hands over his firm wet body, exploring parts that she had previously only imagined. She waited as long as she could, and then she intentionally found his large erection. As expected, it was a mind-blowing turn on. Their bodies were writhing with passion and desire for each other.

The shower was small and felt too restrictive and awkward to complete their lovemaking. Without speaking, they both stepped out of the shower, wrapped in each other's arms. Shuffling in unison and dripping wet—and leaving moist foot marks and small puddles everywhere in their path—they stumbled their way to the bedroom, never missing a beat nor breaking contact. Wrapped in each other's arms, they passionately kissed, caressed and touched each other, hungry for satisfaction and eagerly wanting each other and the culmination of their desire.

Neither one wanted to participate in much foreplay, as they had waited close to six months to have each other, and have each other they did. George couldn't wait any longer. He wanted her and wanted to give her his best. In seconds, moving in unison, their worlds exploded.

Ruby's orgasm was like lifting her mind, body and soul up—up—up into space, taking her breath away. She gasped for air but didn't want to breathe for fear she would lose the momentum. Still holding her breath, she waited to reach the top ... soon now ... soon ... almost there ... then there was a most amazing explosion inside her that sent her to the most astounding heights, with that special spot at the top of her vagina pulsating and pulsating. The sensation was so strong it seemed to lift her head off the bed.

She moaned and groaned, hugged him and whispered into his ear. She expressed her ultimate pleasure. Then slowly, ever so slowly, like an abandoned feather, she floated back to reality with the warmest spectacular glow inside and out. She was huffing and puffing, trying to catch her breath while she truly enjoyed the afterglow.

They both experienced the most madly passionate and erotic sex, again and again. Each one climaxed several times before, totally exhausted, they rolled over, lying on their backs gasping for air, just trying to get sufficient oxygen in their deflated lungs.

George recovered first and kiddingly said through quick breaths, "Next ... time ... we'll do it better."

Ruby chuckled and responded with a mischievous happy contented grin that lit up her whole face. "It was perfect. I don't how we could have done it any better. That was the best sex I have had in many years, maybe ever."

George said, "I have an idea. Why don't we give this hard-working soldier a name?" He pointed to his limp spent penis. This is when they decided to name it "Xmas," because it delivered such delightful gifts, each and every time.

Ruby expressed her inner thought out loud: "What a great way to start my new life."

They lay there wrapped in each other's arms. They joked and laughed about the highs and lows of the day's activities. Actually, there were no lows.

George noticed the bruises on her body and gently kissed them to make them better. They snuggled, holding each other close for most of the night. They both wanted and needed to be comforted by a kind and loving person.

"George, I have something to tell you. Jason, my ex had Herpes, and STD (Sexually Transmitted Disease). Just before I left he forced me to have unprotected sex with him. I have been tested and do not have it. I should have told you last evening but we were both so aroused I decided not to tell you then, but I feel like I should tell you. Just in case you developed symptons or want to get tested."

"Thank you for your honesty. I will consider what you've confessed. The fact that you have been tested but tested negative for Herpes. I'll make my decision later."

George left very early in the morning. He had to go to his apartment for a much-needed shower and a change of clothing. Just before he climbed out of bed, he whispered in her ear, "I'm sure you have no idea how much I care for you. I enjoyed last evening so much."

Sleepily she responded, "Me too."

"Next time, I'll definitely come prepared with fresh clothes for my sleepover." He hadn't thought to bring his toiletries with him. "I promise, next time I'll be better prepared. See you at the office, my lovely."

Ruby dressed for work and ate breakfast in the quiet but welcome loneliness of her new home. She had great memories this morning after that amazingly passionate evening with George the night before.

When Ruby arrived at work, the first thing on her to-do list was to inform her boss of her new status. Entering his office, she said, "Mr. Wilson, I wanted you to be the first to hear this. Not that I plan to make an announcement, but you know we have a very active gossip line here. The reason I wanted yesterday off was because I left my husband." She paused for a moment to gather her composure, and then she continued. "My feelings are too raw right now to go into any details. So if we can just leave it at that for the time being, I would appreciate the space."

Mr. Wilson was maybe 55 or 60 years old, 5 feet 8 inches tall and 140 pounds soaking wet. His clothes were at all times coordinated and nicely tailored. His meticulous salt-and-pepper hair was always carefully blow-dried like he had just exited a hair salon. He was well educated, and he knew his stuff when it came to human resources. In one conversation, he had told Ruby that this was his last position before he retired. He lived locally, and he would be there until the end of his career.

He raised his eyebrows questioning her statement but only asked, "When you can, I would appreciate knowing the circumstances."

Ruby offered him a few small details, saying, "My husband is a monster. I have tried very hard and creatively to hide the evidence of just how abusive he has been for years."

Mr. Wilson asked, "Do you need time to find a place or take care of any personal matters?"

"No, thank you. I moved into an apartment yesterday down near Falcon Mall. That's what I did yesterday on my vacation day. I'm pretty well settled in, but it may take a few weeks to actually get used to being on my own and going home to an empty house every night. At least, I will be safe and free of *him*."

"Well, you let me know if you need any help, anything at all," he sincerely offered.

Ruby struggled to stretch her income and manage her expenses. She made large batches of a really healthy soup that lasted six or seven days. With her tight budget, these soups were her staple for several months until she got caught up with the expense of moving and making this new home *her* new home.

After work, she often felt uncomfortable going directly from work to home. She dreaded going into the deadly quiet lonely apartment. One of her solutions was to wander around the local mall window-shopping for an hour or so first. Finances were tight. Shopping for new clothes was out of the question. She had to keep reminding herself that this was a sacrifice worth making for freedom.

Another solution to help with the loneliness of going home to an apartment absent humans was to meet one or both of her sons for an inexpensive dinner. Once they got used to the idea of their mother living there, they would come for a meal at her new home. She learned very quickly to appreciate her new life. It was quite wonderful. There was no one to abuse her here.

She made some promises to herself:

- Never would she be a victim again.
- Never would she put up with crap from any man ever again.
- Never again would anyone confuse her with a victim.

Her knowledge became her power. Lessons learned became her power.

Her new power changed her and how she was treated by others. *I'm in charge of myself, for better or worse*, she vowed.

Jason phoned several times that week and for weeks thereafter, pleading with her to let him come and see her so they could make love.

"Love? You mean sex, don't you? Well, forget it. It will never happen."

"But Ruby, I still love you."

Ruby, with disgust, emphatically stated, "I have no interest in having a relationship, sex, or anything else with you, so *please* stop calling me."

He persisted with his bootie calls. Ruby got call display and let his calls go to the message machine. She never listened to his messages, just deleted them all.

Ruby believed that Jason didn't want to cause too much trouble for fear he would push her too far and she might lay charges against him or write a tell all book and destroy him. Ruby certainly could cause him problems. Unfortunately she had no proof that would hold up in court.

Jason stalked a woman he had interest in. She wasn't as timid as Ruby. This other woman laid a complaint against him. A judge sent him to jail for 7 days.

Ruby had put up so with much from Jason for so many years she didn't care to see, hear or speak to him ever again. She was finally free of him and his abusive behaviour.

Chapter 26
1979 Continued

George and Ruby ate dinner together at her new apartment on her first free Friday night. She cooked a very special meal: chicken Florentine. It consisted of chicken breasts on a bed of spinach, covered with a delicious hollandaise sauce and then baked, covered, for about fifty minutes.

George brought the wine. He said, "Not only can I sleep over tonight, but we can have a lazy Saturday because I'm armed with my sleepover bag, and I don't have Tammy this weekend."

Perfect, thought Ruby. *This evening will be even better than Monday because we both are more organized. We won't have the first-time jitters either. The sex was great Monday; who knows what's next?* She got horny just thinking about the pleasure she was certainly going to have that night. *Maybe we could have a quickie while dinner is baking? Wow, with these tingles going on in my groin and vagina, I don't think I can wait. I'll never be able to sit still to eat dinner.*

She smiled at George and said, "I can think of something better to eat, and it isn't even fattening."

"Me too."

"George," she said as she walked toward him. "I'm feeling like we should test Xmas and see if he's still performing to our liking and then have dinner. We have time. We have all of the time we want."

George leaned down and planted his mouth on her welcoming parted lips. "Oh, baby," he said. "You're reading my mind. I think I'm addicted to you. Yes, come with me." He took her hand and led her down the hall and into their "love room." She reached over and quickly pulled down the bedding. He gently lay her down on the fresh-smelling sheets. The lovers hurriedly fumbled as they undressed each other.

Buttons—why are they so difficult at moments like this? was the thought that flashed through Ruby's mind as her hands shook from sexual excitement and anticipation.

George, with his immense heightened desire, was uncoordinated; he also fumbled. "Oh my god, my zipper is stuck," he said as she pulled the jammed zipper, almost ripping off his trousers. They were aching to have their satisfaction and to give each other the best time of their lives.

Finally naked and writhing with desire, he mounted her and plunged his enormous cock into her moist vagina. Almost immediately, Ruby's body and mind exploded. She was sure she saw fireworks at the height of her orgasm. George, now fully coordinated, climaxed in unison with Ruby. Breathing heavy and gasping for air, they rolled over and lay there trying to recover.

"Wow, that was fantastic—bloody fantastic" was his cry, as he had conquered his wild sensuous partner.

"Is it my imagination, or is it really getting more mind-blowing every time? *Wow*," Ruby groaned, still enjoying the infamous aftershocks.

"I think you're right, my lovely. If our sex gets much more powerful, I'll have to get oxygen to keep beside the bed so I can revive us." George was pleased with himself. "You know, I can honestly say I'm so glad I waited for you. You are an amazing lover. Thanks, my pretty lady."

Ruby, with wobbly legs, grabbed a robe from behind her bedroom door and toddled off toward the kitchen to check on the baking food. "Dinner's ready whenever you are," she called down the hall.

George's response was, "I'll just take a quick shower. You can join me if you wish."

"If I do, I might just as well put the dinner in the refrigerator until later. I think this time, I will shower when you're done. I don't trust myself in the shower with you. I'll leave you a glass of wine to sip while you wait for me." She knew better than to tempt fate.

They were so attracted to and infatuated with each other. They had trouble keeping their hands off each other's bodies. *The worse is at work—the no-touch zone*, she thought. *Some days my fingers just ache to touch him during coffee breaks or lunch.*

It had become their habit to playfully tease each other during dinner. This served as their foreplay for the next romp in the sack.

George whispered, "I have a special present for you. When you're ready, just let me know."

Ruby reached over to his lap. Smiling, she seductively said, "You certainly do. I'm ready whenever you are. This is going to be a great dessert. Shall we move to the boudoir? We can have the dessert I prepared later. I very much prefer the dessert you have for us."

They were clean from their earlier showers. They each carried their wine and headed to their love nest. With great pleasure, they once again feasted on each other's bodies, this time in a more controlled and less frantic manner. She loved the pleasure his beautiful large cock gave her. She would suck and massage him until he felt like he would lose it and cum too soon.

George was fascinated with her full, succulent breasts. "Ruby, those hard nipples of yours are shouting to me, 'Suck me, please suck me.'"

"Then do what you're told," she replied.

They explored every crevice of each other's bodies, kissing and licking with delight, giving and receiving pure sexual pleasure.

Eventually, he plunged his huge erect cock deep, deep inside her primed vagina. Pure erotic earth-shattering desire engulfed them as they rode the crest of the wave to their orgasm and climax in unison.

During Ruby's orgasm, it felt like the earth shook. Her orgasm was like a going up a roller coaster up ... up ... up ... then she seemed to sit on top of the highest point, feeling wonderful and holding her breath ... waiting ... just waiting for that moment of intense magnificent pleasure to explode. The explosion made her whole body tense up with a shuddering orgasm. She floated in that wonderful place of glorious nothingness like a skydiver drifting through space. Then falling from the sky like a feather caught in a light breeze, she floated to the ground slowly ... slowly ... ever so slowly, drifting in and out ... in and out of wonderful sensuality toward reality. Her whole body went limp while the good-feeling hormone, serotonin, flooded through her veins.

She tried to recover by panting to catch her breath. Her body tingled from the top of her head to the tip of her toes. She flexed her leg muscles. This amazing feeling, as expected, was always followed by pulsating aftershocks that took her up soaring like an eagle to the pinnacle and then down, and then up again and again, jolting her to her core and prolonging her absolute and complete pleasure. She was totally drained and numb all over. Her legs were weak. She wouldn't dare try to stand up with such a light head and wobbly legs. They lay there contentedly holding hands and enjoying the joy they gave each other.

They made beautiful amazing love for quite some time. "Merry Christmas," George said with his chest inflated as his ego took full credit for her colossal ecstasy.

Their appetite for each other was insatiable. Ruby secretly wondered if she was being rewarded for enduring the abuse from Jason until the boys had grown up and left home.

Chapter 27

Life Now A New Normal

Five days after Ruby moved out, her old next-door neighbour from the other part of their semi-detached house, Jenny, telephoned her. Once they got past the usual salutations and catch-up details of the big move, Jenny—eager to share her tidbit of gossip—said, "Ruby, Jason invited a lady and her children to stay for the weekend at the house. Her kids told me that Jason has been dating their mother for quite some time. The kids know 'Uncle Jason' really well."

Ruby smiled and confidently said, "Jenny, thanks for the call, but she can have him. If she stays with him long enough, she'll see the real person—the monster I've lived with for a very, very long miserable time. I'm free. Jason can do whatever he wants, just as long as he stays away from me." Wanting to change the subject, she asked, "How are you doing?"

"I'm good—busy as usual. I've just been promoted to birthing nurse. Good job, but as usual, more evening, night and weekend shifts."

"Congratulations, Jenny. You are so good at your job. Your promotion doesn't surprise me."

"I won't keep you," Jenny said. "I just wanted to tell you about his girlfriend."

"I understand, and I appreciate the call. I'm looking forward to having you come to my new digs for a glass of wine or dinner."

"Great," said Jenny. "I look forward to keeping in touch with you. Thanks. Oops—patient calling. Got to take this. Talk soon."

"Me too. Gotta go."

Ruby disconnected the call. Smiling to herself, she thought, *I don't want to spoil my time with George, so I'll save this little tidbit for later.*

Matt and Joey were frequent visitors at her new apartment, sometimes with their girlfriends. It was easier being an attentive mother when happiness was a daily state of mind. They constantly told her that they were pleased to see their mother free of her abuser.

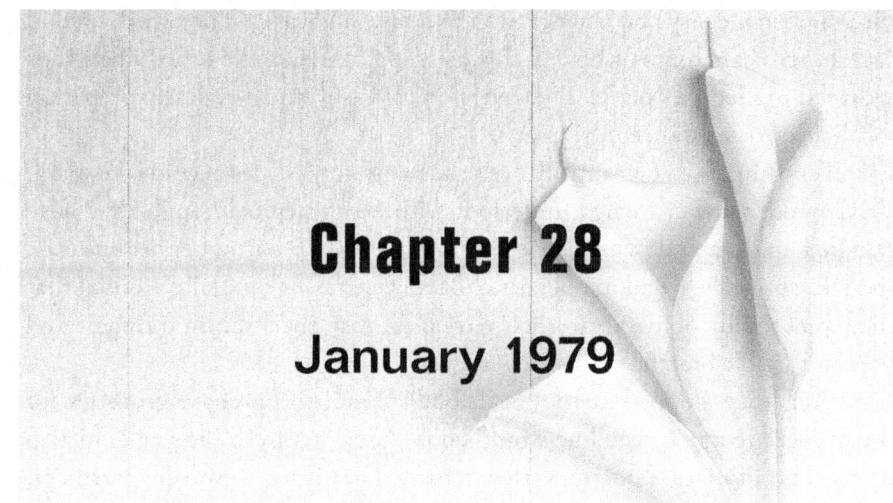

Chapter 28
January 1979

Saturday morning was all about chatting and relaxing while enjoying a hot cup of java on the sun-filled balcony. Breakfast consisted of fruit, eggs and bacon, followed by a shower and more hot—oh so very hot—sex.

Once they recovered from their new ritual, George suggested that they spend the day at his place. It was more secluded, and they were less likely to meet anyone from work. They had to be careful, as both really needed to keep their jobs.

They both drove their own cars to George's new apartment. That way, Ruby could leave on her schedule and go grocery shopping on the way home. She liked the sound of that.

This was Ruby's first time seeing George's apartment. She surveyed each of the rooms and thought, *It is still very sparsely furnished. The bed we'll make love on is a mattress on the floor. Classy! I wonder where Tammy sleeps now when she visits her dad.* She saw that his clothes were still in cartons lined up along the wall. *He does have an entertainment system—probably the most expensive item in the whole apartment.*

She teased, "It doesn't look like you cook much, as there's only one saucepan, a coffee pot and a toaster. A set of dinnerware for four seems to be the full extent of your dishes."

"It works for the limited entertaining I do," he replied.

She thought, *Makes perfect sense. Like most separated men, he's looking for a woman to fill the void the wife left. Maybe that's not a fair comment in George's situation. I don't feel like I'm filling in for anyone.*

That afternoon, they walked hand-in-hand along the bluffs, drinking in the amazing scenery and listening to the pounding waves. They whispered in each other's ears hints of how each was going to please the other when they returned to George's place. They were emotionally and physically preparing for their next sex dance in the sack.

Everything was so beautiful, even the many gray shades of cold lake water. Crisp white snow crunched underfoot with every step. Although they were bundled up in their down-filled winter jackets to keep warm, neither one even thought about the frigid temperature. Both were now so sexually aroused that they were totally oblivious to their red noses, rosy cheeks, numb fingers and toes and visible breath.

Later, they stopped at the local food market to purchase groceries for the dinner George insisted he would cook. Carrying fresh broccoli, chicken breasts and miniature potatoes, they returned to his toasty warm apartment.

They drank wine from water glasses, little knowing that this was becoming a new trend for yuppies. They were ahead of the trend by default. George showed off his domestic skills by cooking a delicious gourmet meal. While eating his masterpiece, they held hands across the table, chatted and listened to his stereo. Under the table, her shoeless toes found his junk. She wiggled her toes, caressing him to full arousal. Concentration on any other topic became difficult.

Both were huge fans of Neil Diamond. Every song he sang was erotic and became their favourite. Years later, every time Ruby heard Neil Diamond sing "Forever in Blue Jeans," she smiled at the memories it churned up. She felt that wonderful tingle in her vagina and wetness between her legs. The memory lived on.

Once again, George offered his special dessert. "Enough," he pleaded. "Let's hit the sack before we explode." The horny couple left the dirty dishes on the table. Ambling down the hallway arm in arm, they moved in unison, kissing and whispering what they wanted from their sex mate. They started with tender, sweet, lovingly soft foreplay. They took their time and enjoyed every erogenous zone.

Then they passionately made love—touching and kissing eyelids, eyebrows, temples, shoulders, hands, arms and hair. Hungrily they touched and stroked each other's zones. This stimulated both Ruby and George and increased their arousal level to territory they never knew existed. Once again, he penetrated her with his very large stiff cock. He was so large that he completely filled her. He was touching all sides of her vagina, and then he hit the G-spot, sending her up, up, up into her favourite space. Her orgasm was like being blasted out of a cannon, up—up—up into oblivion. She held her breath and enjoyed the wonderful feelings that caused her to moan with pleasure.

She arched her back and waited while she seemed to hover in that wonderful place of glorious erotic nothingness, like being suspended in space, and then slowly, ever so slowly, she floated in and out, in and out toward reality. Totally drained, with every inch of her skin tingling, Ruby felt weak as a young sapling. As usual, along came the pulsating aftershocks—up to the pinnacle, then down, then up again and down again. Her whole body tensed and then shuddered each time. She was totally depleted of energy when it was over. As usual, it was difficult for her to catch her breath.

Once again his penis, Xmas, had delivered a delightful gift, as it had each and every time before. It was the gift that just kept on giving.

George, while playfully twisting her hair around his fingers and nibbling her earlobes, said, "I really enjoy making love to you, Ruby. I know I'm sounding like a broken record, but it's true. I've never known anyone to experience such intense climaxes. I'm officially naming your orgasm the "super-duper O."

Ruby shyly smiled and said, "I'm amazed at how erotic our lovemaking time has become. I've reached new heights even for me. I guess it must be Xmas, if we can give credit to anyone or anything." She pointed to his now very limp member. "These orgasms are not going to be easy to forget. Sometimes I wonder if you're spoiling me for any future lover."

They slept wrapped up in each other's arms, offering comfort and support as usual.

Chapter 29
Summer 1979

Janet McNeil, a member of the marketing department, resigned. As was the custom—especially in this creative department, as they were very social—her fellow workers arranged a farewell party. All departments were invited.

Mr. Wilson approached Ruby and asked, "Will you be the representative of the human resources department at the function for Janet?"

"Sure, I can do that," Ruby agreed.

"You know the rules, right? No fraternizing with employees. I'm a real stickler for the implementation of that policy," Mr. Wilson reminded.

Ruby wondered if this was a warning. *Do they know something? Both George and I have always been so very careful around the office.*

Later that morning she saw George in the cafeteria. He asked, "Are you planning to go to Janet's party this Friday?"

"Yes, as a matter of fact I am. Mr. Wilson is sending me as the representative of our department. He also gave me a pep talk about the company's no fraternization policy," she offered with a mischievous smile and twinkle in her eye. She sarcastically said, "I wouldn't think about doing something that would break the fraternization rules." They both grinned and snickered.

"I guess that means we'll not be allowed to dance or sit together at the same table," he teased with a playful grin and a wink.

"You got that right. He and his buddy the president will be watching me like a hawk. I get the impression that he suspects something, but he's not quite sure yet. It may be just because I'm now single that he's anticipating a problem." She looked off into space to mentally review their office behaviour. They had been very careful.

"Can we meet after the party?" he pushed.

"No. I absolutely do not want that to happen. I do not want to have that possibility floating around in the air. I will leave on my own and go home on my time. It'll be better for both of us. We need to be smarter than them."

At the party, Ruby circulated. Wine in hand, she approached a group of coworkers. "Hi, Shirley. How are you doing? Do you still like your new job in the sales department?"

"I love it. So nice to get away from reception. I did like it, but this job is so much better."

Ruby turned and addressed another coworker. "Elaine, good to see you at a function!"

"My kids are older now," Elaine said with a smile. "It's wonderful to have 'latch-key kids.' Mom gets more freedom."

Many females in the group were young mothers. They all smiled and nodded in agreement.

Ruby started to move away. "Great to see you all. I guess I should keep moving—I'm on a mission, as I'm the human resources ambassador. Enjoy!"

A chorus of goodbyes and good nights followed Ruby.

Suddenly, Jack from sales grabbed Ruby and pulled her onto the dance floor.

"Wow! I guess you want to dance, Jack."

"Sure do. I love to dance to any of the Beatles." Jack a very good dancer, really knew how to cut a rug.

Three tunes later, Ruby begged, "Can we sit this one out, please? You're wearing me out."

"Sorry, Ruby. I had a feeling you were a good dancer. Thanks! You're such a good sport." He walked her to a table where some managers were drinking and chatting.

"Ruby, good for you. You lasted longer with Jack than most would have," Merle said, complimenting Ruby while patting her shoulder.

"Yes. He's a high energy character, for sure," said Sean, a sales representative.

"Where's our manners? Have a seat and recover from the gymnastics that Jack put you through. Come sit here." J. D. said as he pulled out a chair for Ruby.

The group laughed, partly from J. D.'s comments, but probably from a few too many alcoholic drinks as well.

George approached the table, leaned in and directed his comment to his peers but more to Ruby. "I'd ask Ruby to dance, but I think she not only needs but deserves a drink to quench her thirst." With that, he placed a glass of white wine in front of her.

Merle teased, "Smooth, George."

More laughter followed.

The party was a lot more fun than this type of get-together normally was. Ruby, now bored with the drunken jokes and phony laughter, said her goodbyes and left. "Night all."

At home, Ruby checked her messages. Jason had called three times, with each call more rude and abusive than the one before. *Delete. Delete. Delete.*

A few hours later, George appeared at her apartment. He was slightly inebriated. Ruby welcomed him with open arms, as she was horny and hoping he felt the same.

Chapter 30

Summer 1979 Cont'd

Monday morning after the farewell party for Janet, Mr. Wilson invited Ruby into his office to have a coffee with him. "How was Janet's send-off?" he asked.

Ruby was taken aback by the question. She responded with caution, "It was okay. I'm not really in a partying mood these days. I'm still adjusting to my new status," she lied.

"I hear you and Jack from sales put on a bit of a show."

"Did I do something wrong?"

"No. I guess I didn't know you could dance like that."

"I'm separated. I didn't join a nunnery."

"Now that you're separated, I don't want to see or hear that you're seeing one of our male employees socially. You know how I feel about office relationships," he stated, reinforcing his previous warning.

"Understood," she responded with an inquisitive frown.

"Mr. Fischer told me this morning that he thought you were a little chummy with one of the male managers in accounting. He also noticed that you totally ignored George in purchasing. Now we all know with George's extrovert personality, that's hard to do," he continued, closely observing her for a hint of a reaction. "The boss man thinks that could be a sign that something is brewing."

"You mean that wonderful man who came to wish the staff in our department happy holidays and shoved his tongue down my throat? Is that the perfect Mr. President you're saying is judging me and my behaviour?"

She got angry every time she thought about their president. More than that, she wanted to change the direction in which their conversation was headed.

"What are you saying? He did that to you? Why didn't you tell me?" Mr. Wilson declared in a very angry voice. With great force, he slammed down his ceramic coffee cup on his desk. The hot coffee spilled onto the glass protector. Much to Ruby's surprise, he was genuinely infuriated and taken aback. She was positive by his reaction he had no idea about his boss's behaviour. *Why didn't he know? Everyone else did!*

"If I had told you, we would have been having this conversation many months ago." She knew she had said too much. It didn't matter; it was clear to her that she was on her way out.

A few weeks passed. She felt the tenseness growing around her. Ruby was not sure what to expect, but something was in the wind. She was sure of it.

Ruby was careful to not add to the negative mood by telling Mr. Wilson about their president and the vice president of marketing telling a secretary a crude joke. Just as Ruby passed by, she heard "rape," and then they laughed. She stopped in her tracks and interrupted. "Both of you fellas have wives and daughters. What is so funny about rape? Would you still find it amusing if a female in your family was raped?" She didn't wait for a response. She just left the comment hanging.

Andre, the vice president of marketing, didn't speak to Ruby for months after that. He always put on a Santa suit and handed out the gifts under the Christmas tree at the office party. Ruby overheard him asking her assistant if she would perform the task this year. Ruby walked out of her office and said, "I will."

Sometime after she had left for the day, Santa's suit and accessories were dropped on her desk. "Perfect." She had a plan.

The day of the office Christmas party, Ruby dressed in her version of Santa. She appeared at the party in costume.

Andre was taken aback when he saw her and asked with a wrinkled nose and disdain in his voice, "Who are you supposed to be?"

Ruby stood tall and proudly declared. "Mrs. Claus." She wore the red hat and fur trimmed red jacket with a wide shiny black belt. Instead of pants, she wore a black skirt with the faux boots. She observed his slow burn and enjoyed every second.

Most of the employees applauded. Point made.

From then on, he called her a feminist. He thought it was a negative or insulting comment. Ruby didn't. She took it as a compliment.

Chapter 31

1980: On the Move Again

Ruby had just settled into her daily routine of processing this week's pay increases. It was a beautiful sunny warm day following a great fun-filled weekend with George.

Mr. Wilson crossed the hall and knocked on her open office door. "Good morning, Ruby. May I come in and have a chat with you?"

"Yes, of course. There's nothing too pressing right now. I have three interviews scheduled for this afternoon."

He entered, closed the door and sat down. He leaned forward, resting his elbows on the top edge of her large wooden desk.

This is different. I wonder what he has on his mind. I really shouldn't be so suspicious. Can't help it—it's in my DNA.

"How was your weekend? Any problems I should know about?" he asked, struggling to sound casual.

Why is he beating around the bush? I'm pretty sure I know his agenda.

"Good. How was yours?" she responded, still wondering what exactly he was up to, as this was not his normal morning routine.

"Do you remember that conversation we had a couple of weeks ago about your career?" he asked, trying to act like he had her best interest at heart.

Ruby was wary about this question. "Sure. Do you have something to add?" She was careful, as this seemed to be unnatural and puzzling territory.

"I just wanted to let you know that you can use me as a reference. I will give you an excellent recommendation and help you find a suitable position. I know lots of people in the recruitment business. I don't mind making a few inquiries on your behalf," he added enthusiastically.

Out of Silence

"I'm not sure. I'm just not very comfortable with this conversation," she warily added. Ruby was asking herself, *Why? Where did this all come from? Is it a coincidence that he's offering his help? No. The big boss wants me out of here. Got it!*

"Don't worry. These conversations often happen in management situations." He attempted to reassure her that all was well and normal.

"You're aware that I have just made a fresh start to my life and in a new home away from my abusive ex-husband. A new position wouldn't go amiss. I do need to be very careful, though." She was paving the way for her next move while helping him with his awkward situation. "So what's going on, Mr. Wilson? Do you have a mandate to encourage me to move on?" She stared directly into his dark brown eyes. She was sure she could tell if he lied to her.

"You're a smart girl," he said, and then he stood and reached for the doorknob. His parting words were, "Remember, I will be happy to give you a great reference."

Ruby thought, *Screwed by a male once again. When will this ever stop? Most likely not in my lifetime.*

That evening, she shared the conversation with George. "Bastards!" was his only repeatable comment.

"Okay, babe," she said. "Let's go play squash." Her new passion for living and her handsome young lover were quickly bolstering her self-esteem.

"But ... you, said ... oh, I get it now. How about tomorrow after work at the club down the street from the office? I'm in for the game. I prefer to play by my rules, though." George didn't hesitate, but he also wasn't sure he was ready to change his employment.

George was already a member of the New You Fitness Club. She signed up for the whole program, squash and fitness. It was time to get her body in shape for a job search.

He had taught her to play squash so they had a sport they could do together. They would go through their fitness routine and then have a game of squash. They played frequently at *their* club. Her apartment complex also offered courts for renters and their guests. The location made playing on weekends less of a hassle.

Cooling off with a cold drink after a rather vigorous match, Ruby said, "It's always the female who needs to leave. You're fine, George. Don't worry. They won't fire you, as they know I'll be leaving soon. I think if I actually applied to be a president, they would give me a glowing recommendation," she teasingly said, grinning from ear to ear. They both had a good laugh.

"Wow, how did you figure that out? Being a woman requires a whole other set of skills."

"You have no idea," she boldly responded.

She deserved this new life. She had paid her dues. Her professional credentials were current, and her body at the age of thirty-nine was in its best shape ever.

Watch out, world. Ruby Monroe is in the game.

It was important to her that she acquire new and secure employment. She couldn't survive without a reliable steady income. Every day, she scoured the want ads. Not a single advertisement suited her skill set. She also signed up with agencies that placed people in open positions. Her resumé was excellent and demonstrated her continuous increased responsibility and accountability as she moved up the corporate ladder.

She didn't know if it was taking too long to find employment or they were just in a big hurry to have her move on. Apparently, the powers that be—including Mr. Wilson—were getting impatient. Mr. Wilson summoned her into his office and asked her to bring along her resumé.

He said, hand outstretched, "Ruby, I would like to offer my assistance and help you with your job search. Let me see your resumé." Ruby slid it across his desk. He read it then scribbled additional descriptive words that definitely aided in sprucing up her accomplishments and responsibilities. The additions were not lies, just slight exaggerations and probably a better description.

Mr. Wilson returned her resumé, pushing it back across the glass desktop toward her. "I think you will get some bites now. If you need any more help, just let me know."

"Hmmm! These changes will definitely help make my job search shorter for sure," said Ruby. "More importantly, on paper, I appear to be far more qualified for better jobs within my area of experience and qualifications. I guess I tend to be more conservative about my depth of knowledge. Thanks. I appreciate your help."

To her surprise, Mr. Wilson also suggested, "Ruby, to make your job search easier for you, I think you should accept interviews during the business workday. I'll cover for you." Ruby left his office with mixed feelings. *I wonder if I'll be able to find a really good suitable job in their secret time frame. Also, just how much time do I actually have? Money is really important to me, being the only breadwinner. I would never choose a job based on only money, but a healthy salary is critical.*

The easier my boss makes it for me, the more convinced I am that they, management, for some reason unknown to me, want me out, and soon. Maybe their problem is my feminist attitude? This new bolder take-no-crap-from-anyone approach put her in control.

Driving home, Ruby reviewed the events of the day in her head. *Yep! I'm sure I'm right. The writing is already on the wall. I think it would be prudent of me to move quickly, especially when they're offering so much assistance in my job search.*

Chapter 32

1980: Moving On

Spring and summer with George were the most wonderful times of her life. They played serious competitive squash a couple of times a week, sometimes more frequently. It was great exercise, they were together, and let's face it—the sex after such invigorating exercise was truly *amazing*.

Ruby looked forward to visits from Matt and Joey. Matt had just returned from a hippie-type trip abroad. He traveled via Euro Rail or hitchhiked throughout Europe and the Middle East. Afterward, he stayed in his mother's spare bedroom until he found other accommodations, and he shared some of his adventures with Ruby. One in particular made her happy that she heard the details *after* he arrived home.

"Mom," said Matt. "I didn't dare tell you when this actually happened, but I'm home now so I feel that I can share this with you. One day, I rode on a small school-style bus from one town to another, ending in Tehran. I wanted to rest my feet after a long day of walking, so I was about to remove my boots. The bus driver said, 'If I were you, I wouldn't take my boots off during the overnight trip.'

"I naïvely asked, 'Why? My feet are tired.'

"'Most likely, they will not be still on the bus in the morning,' was his response.

"When we got to Tehran and exited the bus, there were several soldiers standing there with machine guns pointed at our guts."

Ruby exclaimed, "Oh my God, Matt!" She immediately ran to her son and hugged and hugged him.

"I'm okay," Matt assured her. "It was dramatic for sure, but it turned out to be a non-event. Although I will never forget the adrenalin jolt when I saw the machine guns."

"When did this happen?" she asked.

"Around the time the US ambassador and staff had been taken hostage. The Canadian embassy played an important part in them being rescued. Thank goodness, or things might have been worse."

Ruby was still in shock. "If I had my way, I would never let you go there again."

"I've got more stories to tell you, but right now I'm tired. I need some sleep. See you in the morning."

"Good night, Matt. I'm glad you're safe and at home."

She felt like they were a family again. Except for the annoying "telephone sex" calls from Jason she received from time to time, life was good.

Frequently, George, Ruby, and his daughter, Tammy, played Frisbee together. Their antics sent them into fits of laughter, with playful jostling and gentle playful pushing and shoving. When it came to Frisbee, George was so very coordinated, and Ruby was a total klutz. Tammy giggled as she ran up and down under the Frisbee. She reached up with her little arms desperating trying to touch the Frisbee that she could never have caught. *This game has proved to not be one of my strong skills,* she thought. They all jogged together when Tammy was present George jogged with her on his shoulders. They exercised until they were totally exhausted.

Every second weekend, she and George picnicked with Tammy, and with Matt and Joey when they were available. The boys really liked George, and he liked them. Sometimes on off weekends, Ruby met with girlfriends or her boys. When Ruby and George could arrange a picnic for two, that was the order of the day. They always walked hand in hand or with arms wrapped around each other. They did all of those fun things that young lovers do.

Ruby was now 40 years old and trying to keep up with a younger and stronger 30-year-old. This required her to work very hard at their outdoor physical activities.

I know I can almost keep up with him. Not on the squash court, though, as he is so much stronger and taller than me. The thought did occur to her that maybe he was just letting her think she was keeping up. She smiled at his kindness. *Maybe he doesn't want me to feel old and give up. Smart lover I have!*

She hadn't dreaded her fortieth birthday at all. Who would have ever imagined that she would be in the best shape of her life and with such an adoring younger male companion who treated her like his princess and cared so much for her? Ruby truly felt blessed.

She often reminded herself that these days were appreciated more than anyone knew, as she considered them the replacement for the teen years she missed by getting pregnant. Her fun and fancy-free teen years were lost—gone forever. She married and became a mother all at age 16. Back then, there was no time for games.

They were so happy with each other and for the most part absolutely carefree. She hoped nothing would happen to burst their bubble.

Chapter 33

Pushed Out

Ruby now concentrated even more on her job search. With her enhanced resumé, she was open to better jobs that previously she wouldn't have considered. One of the recruitment firms she had signed up with came across a job vacancy they thought would be perfect for her.

"Hi, Ruby. This is Anita from The Job Hunters. Can you talk?"

"Sure. Do you have something for me?" she asked.

"I do. It's a large clothing company. They are in need of a human resources manager to run the salaried employees' section, pay system and benefits. Is this something you might consider?" Anita asked. She shared everything she could until they met in person at the agency's office.

"It sounds very interesting," said Ruby. "I assume the salary is in the range I told you? I must be able to pay my expenses." She didn't want to waste her time if the financial part of the position didn't meet her requirements.

"Yes. You will be very happy with the money. Let's meet. You tell me when—but don't wait too long, as this position will likely go fast."

Ruby knew that a seasoned recruiter like Anita knew a good fit when she saw one—and also that she would savour the commission she could earn if she was successful in finding the right person to fill the vacant position.

They met later that day. Anita was right—the position did appeal to Ruby. An appointment with the employer was immediately scheduled during business hours.

Ruby attended an interview the very next day. She really liked Vince Troth, who would be her immediate supervisor. Her first impression of Vince: *He's a minimalist. Clear desk, no stacked files or clutter.* The only items on his desk were a pad of paper with a few notes scribbled by hand and a pen. Vince carried his fondness of clean lines to his smartly cut suit, crisp white shirt and the geometric design on his tie. He spoke clearly, always smiling. *I really admire his style—plus he comes across as very knowledgeable about his field, human resources.*

Ruby, as any applicant would do, had researched the company. It was stable and doing well in a lucrative market.

She and Vince discussed the duties and responsibilities of the position, plus the reporting structure. Ruby interpreted Vince's comments to mean that he was keen on Ruby and her fit into the company. To seal the deal, Ruby was enticed with the details of the approved succession planning for the position, which included potential future promotion opportunities.

The position had all the bells and whistles—everything she'd ever wanted, including the perfect status for her continued climb up the corporate ladder. She knew she was nowhere near the glass ceiling, but this job would bring her a step or two closer.

As promised, Mr. Wilson provided her with a glowing reference.

Anita, from the search firm, telephoned Ruby the next day to congratulate her and to advise her of the good news. "They want to hire you. If you also agree and wish to accept their offer, I'll send you an employment letter by fax today. This way, you can read it through tonight, and then I'll send an original copy via courier tomorrow to be signed and dated by you," Anita announced with the enthusiasm of someone in line for a big commission.

Ruby, as requested, signed one copy agreeing to all the conditions included and then faxed one signed copy of the employment agreement back to the employer and the other one to the search firm.

Once everything was signed and faxed, she walked into Mr. Wilson's office, sat down and said, "I really do want to thank you for the excellent reference. They offered me the position and I accepted. They would like me to start in two weeks. Will that work for you? Is that enough notice, or did you want me to stay until you find my replacement?"

"No, that's fine," he said. "It'll likely take more than two weeks to find your replacement. Why don't you take some time today, walk around and say goodbye to your friends?" Her stomach hit bottom. *Why are they rushing me out the door?*

Ruby frowned. She was taken aback, and it showed, "Really? I have some things that I should finish up. I don't like to leave unfinished work."

"You know this is our normal process with managers. Once a manager resigns, we usually encourage that person to leave right away. It really is better for morale. I also want to say that there is no need for you to come back here to work after today."

"Employees are going to think I was fired."

"No. I'll prepare the notice of your resignation and show it to you before I distribute it. Don't worry."

"Okay." Ruby was slightly uncomfortable with the speed of her exit.

"You should take any personal effects you have here when you leave today," he continued. "We'll pay you in full for the normal two weeks' notice period—which, as you know, is our legal requirement. I'll calculate your company pension refund. You shouldn't do that anyway. It wouldn't look right."

"Sure. Whatever works. That will give me time to get more of my personal stuff in order. Thank you so much." Ruby knew the game. She had become quite astute at corporate politics. The topic had become her second favourite pastime. Feminism was now her first. She spent a lot of time reading self-help books about growing into a successful female executive. Her current scenario was all there in print.

The staff did arrange for a farewell party on the following Friday. They bought her a very nice gift. She was presented with a beautiful pewter bowl engraved with the company name, her name and the current year. It seemed like everyone—both salaried and plant hourly employees—were there to wish her farewell and success.

"I'm humbled by the numerous well-wishers here in attendance and those who sent cards and notes. I'm stunned when I look out at the gathering here today—so many faces I will miss. I'm pleased to see the various employees that I include in my circle of positive relationships and friends. Thank you all for taking time out of your personal life to be here."

Even Mr. Fischer, the horny president, put in an appearance just long enough to present her with the gift. She felt herself stiffen with disgust as he gave her a hug and a peck on the cheek, wishing her success with any future endeavours. He was one person she definitely *wasn't* going to miss.

George said, "I want to dance with you and maybe even kiss you while on the dance floor. I'm bitter, and I want to throw it in their face. I know, I know—I still have to work here."

She whispered in his ear, "Let's be bigger than them. I have everything I want. And the bonus is, we don't have to hide our feelings for each other anymore."

Chapter 34
1982: A New Chapter

Ruby loved her new managerial position. The staff was qualified and very welcoming. Her direct reports were pleased to have a female supervisor with the skill to do the job and a willingness to teach them more.

She was delighted with the size of her new office. The furnishings were new, as was the very large cherry-wood double-pedestal desk. When she saw the full wall of windows, she inhaled and exhaled a "Wow." The view of the city was impressive. There was even new gray plush carpeting throughout.

Within the first two weeks, she made a new friend: Lila, a product manager for their leather line.

"Hello, Ruby. I'm Lila. Welcome to Pompous Creations."

"Thanks! It's very confusing for a new person in such a large workspace. I'll figure it out. I'm new to this neighbourhood; I just moved here over the weekend from the east end. What does one do for excitement around here?"

"Personally, I love to play golf and squash," Lila replied. "Do you do either one?"

"I love squash," Ruby told her. "Where do you play?"

"You may not know this, but there are courts in the basement of this building, and the price is right: *free*."

"Good one."

"Also, there is a private-membership squash club at the corner of Simpson and Queen. They have really nice facilities," Lila shared.

"That would work for me. I may use the company's courts in a pinch," said Ruby, "but normally I like to have my leisure activities away from where I work."

"Gotcha! Do you live locally?"

"Yes. My rental is just off Queen Street."

"We both live in the same neighbourhood," Lila noted. "This is good. I'd be happy to show you around."

"Super! Nice talking to you, Lila. You know where my office is better than I do at this point. Call or drop by and tell me when we are playing squash."

"It's a date."

Ruby liked Lila. Both were single gals with feminist ideas. They frequently went out to the local restaurants and bars. They remained good friends for many years.

This was Ruby's first experience working for a family-owned business. The father, Charles Pomp, was chief executive officer, and his two sons each ran a division of Pompous Creations. Walter, the more casual and sports-loving son, ran the sporting clothing line, while Paul, the more cerebral brother, ran the leather clothing and bag line. Both operated under the tight control of their elderly gray-haired father, who had started the business and was now enjoying the fruits of his labour.

Ruby had heard a few negative comments in the past about working for family-owned companies, but nothing negative about this particular one. They treated her like an accomplished manager in her field of expertise, and she was just that.

George arrived at her apartment with a bottle of their favourite wine—pinot grigio—to celebrate Ruby's new management position. He poured two glasses and handed one to Ruby. He raised his glass and then clinked hers. "You did it. I'm not surprised. I always knew you would land on your feet. Congratulations, my lovely."

Ruby was not only excited about her new job, she also wanted to share her latest big event with him. "George, you know how undependable my little Pinto has been, right?"

"Yeah. So what are you telling me?"

"I went to a car dealership last night just to look. They made me a deal I couldn't turn down. A better working car is important now that I'm driving farther to work, and at least half of the time on a very busy highway. I needed a reliable vehicle."

"You bought a new car?" Eyebrows raised with shock, he smiled. He knew how brave this purchase was for Ruby.

"Yep. I don't own it—the bank does. But this is a major step for me as a single woman. I have been approved for a car loan. Can you believe that?"

"Yeah, I guess that is a big deal for you. As a man, I would never even think that I wouldn't be approved. You, my friend, have come a long way."

"I assume that the car was in your name so you didn't need to negotiate with Jason."

"Yes we did that for insurance purposes. The transaction is a bonus."

"I do want to share the rest of this story with you," she said. "Please don't think poorly of me. I took the new car out for a test drive. I liked driving the newer bigger car a lot. They gave me a really good buyout on the Pinto. I did all of the paperwork and, as I said, was approved. I'll pick it up in a couple of days."

She continued, "When I first arrived at the dealership, I drove forward into the spot when I parked my old car. This was a bad idea, as the parking space was right in front of the main entrance to the dealership, and the reverse gear on the Pinto has been very erratic lately. When the deal was done, I got into my car and put it in reverse, but it wouldn't move. So I put it back into park and left it running while I got out of the car, walked to the rear and opened the hatch as if I was looking for something. Once it was sufficiently warmed up, a couple of minutes later, I got back into it, and when I put it in reverse gear, it backed up just fine."

"Why did you do that?"

"If there was anything mechanically wrong with the Pinto, they likely wouldn't have given me such a good trade-in on the car. That would mean I couldn't afford the new one. When I pick up the new car, I'll find a space that I can drive through or back into."

"That was either clever or sneaky."

"A little bit of both, I guess. I giggled about it on the way home. I couldn't believe I did that. A couple of years ago, I would never have had the courage to pull off something like that."

"I have seen the change in you. You're more outgoing and confident. That's a good thing."

"Really, I didn't start out to hide anything from them, but once I was approved, I was afraid they would cancel the deal because that little prank may have been construed as lying. Self-preservation or looking out for me was my only motivation."

Chapter 35

Two months after Ruby's arrival at Pompous Sports, Vince, her immediate supervisor, left the company. He told Ruby that he had found an amazing position that was perfect for him. He said he was comfortable with her ability to fill his shoes.

It never occurred to Ruby to question him further, but later she wondered if they had paved the way for him like her previous company had for her. Regardless, she wasn't sure that his leaving was good news for her.

Nevertheless, knowing that she had landed on her feet and feeling financially secure, Ruby approached Jason about applying for a no-fault divorce. This was how she chose to close that door and move on.

Jason continued to stay in their house for about one year after she left. When their divorce was finalized, they decided to sell the house they had lived in together. When they met at the lawyer's office to sign the closing sale papers, she discovered that Jason had forged her signature on documents to add a $30,000 second mortgage to the original one on their house. Jason had spent the whole amount, so the money had to be repaid with the proceeds from the sale. He had cheated her again.

Ruby didn't care as much as she would have even two years earlier. That chapter of her life was now closed.

The new vice president of labour relations, Mr. Miller, took over Vince's duties. Mr. Miller was about 5 feet 7 inches tall, with a rotund body (probably eighty pounds overweight) and a full head of gray hair. *This is never a good reporting structure for human resources*, thought Ruby. *We fare much better when reporting directly to the most senior executive—definitely not to a person with a labour relations mindset. This move makes me very nervous.*

On Ruby's six-month anniversary, her new supervisor, Mr. Miller—or *the weasel*, as she had come to think of him—sauntered into her office. Most of the staff had left for the day.

He said, "Ruby, would you mind if I sit and have a little chat?"

"Sure. Come in. Have a seat."

With that, he squeezed his oversized body into the visitor chair opposite her. Leaning back in the chair, his fingers intertwined behind his head, he crossed his legs. His cocky mannerisms set off warning signals in her brain. "How's it going, Ruby?" he said.

Like he cares. I wish he had left his enormous ego at the door.

She responded, "Fine. What's the agenda for your little chat? Is there something specific you want to discuss?"

Ruby shuddered as he gave her an *I'm better than you* smirk that screamed, *Wouldn't you like to know. Maybe I have a little surprise for you.* She had never been able to read the man. She just didn't like or trust him. His sneaky sneer made her feel very uneasy.

Then he continued, "You know the career path that Vince said was open for you when he hired you?"

Hesitantly, Ruby said, "Yes. I remember. That is one of the reasons I left my last position to accept this one." She thought, *Red-flag alert. Be still my heart. What is he up to now?*

"Well ..." He started to say something, but then he briefly halted while he surveyed the walls and ceiling of her office. After his pregnant pause, he looked back at her and casually stated, "That career path no longer exists. I have the approval to reorganize the department. I took that position out of the organization chart and created a new, more junior position. It will report directly to me. I need assistance with my labour relations day-to-day reports and activities."

"Really. That's very interesting. Do you have someone in mind?" she asked, but being a people-watcher, she knew who Mr. Miller had been cozying up to lately.

"I'm going to promote Neil, your assistant, to that position. It's a done deal. He starts tomorrow."

Her heart sank, but her gut told her she had to remain calm. She asked,

"Why would you do that? Do I get a say, as he is my assistant? Besides, he is really green, with only six months experience—plus he's right out of school."

"Nope. I know how green he is, but I like him, and he's trainable."

Ruby thought, *You mean mouldable.*

The main purpose of his visit accomplished, he got up from his chair and casually strutted toward the door. At the doorway, he turned to look at her, paused and then said, "Oh, by the way, we never had this conversation."

Where is a recording device when you need one? This would have been a conversation that would have got me a great settlement in a wrongful dismissal case.

With that, he slithered out of her office. He was gone as quickly as he had appeared. His departure left her in shock. She was hurt and angry that he had an arbitrary veto over her career path. She felt violated once again.

A few years ago, she would have cried, commented, or displayed some emotion. Not today. That would not happen—plus, this was not the place. Female managers don't cry. She had developed a tough exterior, and that is all the world would see. Inside, however, she was devastated.

Ruby drove home, trying to concentrate on the drive. She was angry but held her feelings inside her for now. The second she closed her apartment door behind her, however, she allowed herself to shed the tears that had been waiting to flood down her face. She sobbed. *Why me? What did I do to deserve this?*

She had foolishly thought she was in control. She still didn't get it. The upper management—all of them men—played with people's lives like pawns on a chessboard. The organization didn't matter. Ruby had developed a saying: "Different corporation and different men, but the game is always the same."

The next day, she telephoned a recruiter friend. "Hi, Stan. Do you have any HR jobs?"

"No, Ruby. But I think you might want to get out of that company sooner rather than later."

"I can't just quit," she told him. "I'm on my own and need my paycheque to survive."

"Maybe this would help: I'd gladly hire you as a recruiter at my firm. Hell, you could start tomorrow if you wanted to."

"That was not exactly what I expected to hear," Ruby replied, "but I'll think about your kind offer. I don't want the reputation of running away at the first sign of conflict. But one thing's for sure: I'm *not* going to allow them to abuse me, either."

Later the next day, she met with Walter, the son who headed up sports clothing manufacturing. He was a kind and caring type, even though he had the reputation of being a jock. Ruby repeated the complete discussion she'd had with her manager the weasel the day before. "And as he walked out of my office, he said, 'We never had this conversation.' What conversation? He told me what he was going to do. There was no consultation, and certainly no conversation. Walt, is there anything you can do? Am I already past-tense?"

She could see that he was genuinely upset and angry. "I'm so sorry to hear this was handled so poorly," he apologized. Then he added, "I'll look into it, but I don't know what I can actually do about it. It is his department." He did not want to give her false hope.

Ruby told him straight out, "I never want to be someone's pawn. Furthermore, I do not want that weasel to have the satisfaction of thinking I'm desperate and begging for my job." Abruptly, she stood up, as if she'd had a change of mind. She said with the most inner strength she could muster, "Don't bother looking into it. I couldn't work with that weasel after this, now or ever again. But you do realize I have a good case for litigation: sex discrimination."

Walter nodded, his eyes wide.

"Here's my letter of resignation," she said, handing the envelope to Walter as she left his office. She had worded the letter very carefully so as to leave the door open for litigation.

With a strong sense of purpose, Ruby walked quickly through the building, not making eye contact with anyone she met. Back in her office, she held back her tears of anger as she cleaned out her desk. She briefly explained the situation to her staff of five and then said, "I just don't want any of you to think that I'm abandoning you. You guys should be okay. None of you is a threat to Mr. Miller."

Ruby started toward the department's door, and then she turned, smiled and waved goodbye to her staff. Before leaving, she stopped at Neil's desk and said, with as much sincerity as she could manage, "Congratulations on your promotion." Her parting comment to Neil was, "Watch your back. He is throwing you into the fire without the proper training. I'm concerned that he is setting you up for failure. Please be careful, Neil."

Sheepishly, Neil bowed his head. "Thanks. I will be careful. Good luck. I'm sure you'll land on your feet."

Chapter 36

A New Slant on Recruitment

Stan, her recruiter friend, was as good as his word. Ruby immediately joined his executive recruiting group. She had access to all open human resources and management positions, with first dibs on any new HR positions other consultants brought in. This was a gold mine. It was like living in a candy shop. Not only did she have priority access, but she saw the critique of the employer and often the review by the leaving employee of the company. They paid Ruby with a monthly draw. This she needed to live on.

The majority of the consultants' skill sets were suitable for sales representatives. That's what recruitment specialists in this type of company really were. Ruby, through education and training seminars, had developed a much more unique set of professional skills. She felt like this company would not be her home for long. Ruby successfully placed three managers and therefore was able to pay back her monthly draw, plus she had enough money to pay her bills.

Stan had asked Ruby to prepare a presentation, which she invited all of the consultants to attend. The subject was "Recruitment"—her specialty. It was payback to her friend for being there for her. Stan and the consultants expressed their appreciation for the inside knowledge Ruby gave them, which helped them do their jobs better.

One month later, Ruby attended an interview for a position with not only more responsibility but a substantially higher compensation package than the one she had just left. The position was at Mix and Match Cosmetics. It pleased her that this wonderful new job was located just five minutes from her apartment. She was more than qualified for the HR management position.

During her initial interview with the president, he asked, "Do you think you could perform the duties of a labour relations assistant to the vice president, who works out of our head office in Los Angeles?"

Ruby took a deep breath. "Yes, I honestly think I have a good base of experience and education that has prepared me to learn how to do that job—and well." She couldn't believe her ears. Interesting—they wouldn't consider her for labour relations at her last company because she wasn't trained. This company was more than willing to train her.

"I love to learn new things and improve my skills," she said. "Sure, I would like that very much." Ruby responded. *This job is sounding better all the time*, she thought.

"We would like to send you to Los Angeles for assessment and evaluation—all expenses paid for by the company. We will arrange for the flight to and from, plus the limo to the hotel and meals. You will stay at a hotel very close to our head office in Hollywood, California."

There was a short pause. *I think he's waiting for me to catch my breath*, she thought.

"Are there any days next week that would not work for you?" She felt that the president was making it clear that she was his favourite applicant.

"My schedule is pretty open," Ruby replied. "I'm working at the recruitment firm on commission. My supervisor knows that I'm looking for something that more closely fits my experience and skills—as a matter of fact, something just like this position. If you book the trip, I will clear my calendar."

When Ruby got into her car for the drive home, she pinched herself. *Stay calm. You're not there yet. One more step. Don't celebrate yet.*

Ruby shared the details of her interview that afternoon with George. She tempered her enthusiasm when she cautioned him, "I'm very nervous. I don't know what to expect next. Why two days of interviews? I don't know. Maybe I won't be successful."

"I have every confidence in you that you will do great," George replied.

"I've not only landed on my feet, but I'll be a member of the senior management committee—plus, and most importantly, I will be reporting to the president. This is an international company with shareholders. No more family businesses for me." She couldn't stop smiling.

George had faith that Ruby would be offered the job. "Sweetie, they are smart people. Look how quickly they acted. You'd have to do something really stupid to lose this job. We both know *that* won't happen."

George and Ruby enjoyed a celebratory drink, dinner and sex—not necessarily in that order or in the singular tense.

The last thing Ruby said to George as she fell asleep was, "I'm so nervous and excited to be going to California for the final interviews. I feel like an up-and-coming executive. That glass ceiling is getting closer." She smiled to herself when she said, "I wonder what it sounds like when the glass ceiling shatters?"

Ruby received a phone call. "Ms. Monroe?"

"Yes."

"Hello, my name is Dana. I'm the president's administrative assistant at Mix and Match Cosmetics. He asked me to make an appointment with you. Would you please drop by the office today and pick up an envelope? I'll be here to go over the details with you."

"Yes, Dana. I will be there at about three o'clock. Is that okay?

"Perfect. I'll be waiting for you."

"Thanks." Ruby wasn't positive the envelope contained a job offer, but she wanted so much to believe she had been successful in getting the job.

Ruby sat in the reception area and read the letter with interest. It began: "We are pleased to offer you the position of Human Resources Manager, conditional on positive feedback from the Management at Head Office in Hollywood." She met with Dana, who explained the details and the expectations of those at the head office.

When Ruby got home, she read the letter several times and then repeated it to herself several more times: "Hollywood … Hollywood, California." *I have never been to California.* The butterflies in her stomach took flight.

Chapter 37

California—Here Comes Ruby

Other than the time of the flights, hotel reservations and instructions on where to be and when, there were no other details written in the letter that mattered. With a puffed-up chest, she felt her confidence growing into an assertive, I'm-in-charge demeanour. She was very confident that she would pass this scrutiny with flying colors.

George provided a note of caution. "Careful, Ruby. Overconfidence can be the enemy. I'm not saying don't be confident, just tone it down a bit so you come across as self-assured and not cocky."

With the three-hour change of time and the length of the flight, it was still daylight when Ruby flew over Los Angeles, a massive city of 10 million people. She was excited and very happy that the company had booked her a window seat so she could see the whole city below her, just waiting for her arrival.

Once at the hotel, she checked in, took her luggage to her room and then hurried down to the lobby. Ruby wanted to explore this new environment.

She asked the uniformed concierge for the name and direction of a restaurant where she could have dinner. His reply took her by surprise. "Madame, I suggest that you have dinner at our Penthouse restaurant. You know, there are some areas that are not safe, especially for women and at this time of night."

She was a stranger, so she followed the doorman's suggestion. It didn't matter that she had to eat in-house. She was, for the first time in her life, right there in the middle of Hollywood, California. This was the number-one most exciting time of her life.

Out of Silence

A couple of times over the past week, Ruby had reflected on her new life. Despite her nervousness, leaving Jason after twenty-two years of marriage and moving into her very own apartment had turned out to be no big deal. *Why did I put up with Jason's abuse for so long? If only I had known everything would work out so great for me, I would have left him sooner—much sooner.*

Both the dinner and the views were fantastic.

The next day was typically Californian: beautiful, bright and sunny. Not that Ruby saw much of the sun. She spent the whole day in interviews.

Interview #1

The vice president of operations asked Ruby many questions about production, determining what she actually knew about this part of the business and how she made her choice in selection of unionized hourly employees for production-line work. He asked, "Ruby what do you think will be your greatest challenge in finding and hiring hourly production employees?"

Ruby confidently responded, "My experience has shown me the best sources for the most qualified hourly employees. I start by implementing good selection processes. Once I've decided the applicant has the experience and skills for the position, I sell the company, working conditions and pay rate to the suitable candidates."

"What about salaried staff, supervisory and management?"

Ruby took a moment to gather and sort out her answer. "There are different sources for plant supervisory personnel than for managerial searching. I have many contacts in the industry. The first question—once the job description, salary and education have been determined—is, do you want someone from the industry or outside the industry."

Two hours later, Ruby was escorted to the next interview. The VP of operations shook her hand and said, "Ruby, I like what I've heard today. Good luck with the rest of your itinerary."

Interview #2

The vice president of financial services chose questions on salary ranges, conducting surveys and calculating benefits. He asked about her experience in budgeting for numbers of people needed for future production requirements. Ruby knew how to answer. Carefully, with details, she explained how she would deal with each situation. She was wearing out and happily accepted a beverage and a snack.

Ruby was relieved that this vice president chose to have a casual chat while they consumed their coffee and muffins. When his time was up, he called his administrative assistant and said, "Karen would you please take Ms Monroe to John Silver's office and introduce them?"

"Certainly. Come with me Ms Monroe."

Interview #3

John Silver, the vice president of sales and marketing, started out by asking, "Ms Monroe, may I call you Ruby?"

"Yes, please."

"I think by now, your brain may be feeling a little strained. How about I tell you about our products and something about our place in the industry?"

"Perfect. I think my tongue could use a rest, and my ears need the exercise."

"Good answer. I've never heard it put that way before, Ruby."

Interview #4

The vice president of public relations, Ron Wilton, led Ruby out of the building and into the underground garage. Ruby wondered where they were going. Before she could ask, he said, "We're going for lunch at the Brown Derby. Do you know the Brown Derby?"

"Only from the movies," she said. They both chuckled.

"Do you have any unanswered questions left over from this morning's itinerary?"

"No," said Ruby. "Everyone was very good at answering my questions. I hope I was as thorough as they wanted me to be in responding to theirs."

"I have not heard a negative comment from anyone. I think you're good."

Over lunch, the questioning began again. Public relations was not something Ruby knew much about, and she told him so.

"Ruby, thank you for your honesty," he replied. "I can tell when someone

BSes me. Tell you what—I'll give you an overview of a few issues that my department has had to resolve with no damage to our reputation."

"That would be very interesting for me. Thank you."

Interviews #5 and #6

The afternoon included interviews with the vice president of human resources and the vice president of labour relations. These were easy for Ruby. She knew her stuff and proved it.

"Ruby, we're pleased with your excellent references and to see that you have obtained certification for your area of expertise," said Jeff Small, the human relations VP. "What does CHRP stand for?"

"Certified Human Resources Professional. I believe you have a similar designation here in the US."

Ruby had done her homework and felt compelled to broach the subject of recruitment and the Canadian Human Rights Act. "You're assessing my suitability for your Canadian office," she continued, "and I believe I will do a great job and will apply all laws that specify when a company located in Canada cannot discriminate against an applicant."

"We're good with abiding with the local employment laws," Jeff responded. "You have extensive laws in your work area. How do you navigate through all those regulations?"

"We have a saying," Ruby told him. "'Don't ask questions you don't need the answer to.' For instance, don't ask a young married woman if she is planning to start a family. Should she respond in the affirmative, HR must have another strong reason for not hiring her, especially if she is qualified for the position. If she is qualified, she has a discrimination claim for not being hired. She could claim that the company didn't hire her because she might get pregnant and take up to six months maternity leave—all at a cost to the company, including hiring a temp replacement and paying her benefits in her absence."

"So don't ask the question, and she doesn't have a case," said Jeff.

"Correct."

"We're depending on you to keep us out of court and legal issues."

"I will do my best to protect both the employees and the company." Ruby knew she scored with her example. She smiled with confidence.

Interview #7

Dinner was the setting for her seventh interview of the day. The president's administrative assistant, Shana, took Ruby to a trendy boutique restaurant. The servings were very small but extremely attractive and pleasing to the taste buds.

Ruby was pleased when she saw the small portions. She had not worked up much of an appetite. In fact, she wasn't hungry at all.

Shana's role was to help Ruby fill in the blanks on any subject she chose. Eventually, Ruby was dropped off at her hotel following a very exhausting day of interviews.

Day #2

The psychological and aptitude testing consumed nearly eight hours of her second day in Hollywood. Before she left the executive offices late on that second day, she was invited to the office of Mr. Redwood, the vice president of labour relations. Ruby would be reporting directly to him for all Union Issues.

"Ruby, I was asked to advise you that the executive committee is going to recommend you. Everyone has been very impressed with your qualifications and interpersonal skills." He continued, "I'm truly impressed with the positive feedback from everyone you spent time with, both yesterday and today. I'm looking forward to working with you. We are confident that you are a well-qualified human resources manager for our Canadian office."

"Thank you," said Ruby. "I also look forward to working with you and your staff. I promise I will do my best to not disappoint."

"I do have one more question for you," said Mr. Redwood. "Why didn't you attend college or a Canadian university?"

"Full disclosure?"

"Yes, please."

"I didn't actually graduate from high school either. I became a mother at age 16. I had to work; we needed the money. I have tried to fill in the blanks by taking courses and completing all the requirements to obtain my professional designation."

"Mr. Branson, the psychologist who administered your tests, said you're a really smart lady. I have your test scores here. You passed everything with the same level of scores as an intelligent US college graduate. Personally, I'm impressed."

"Thank you for the great feedback. I read a lot and took extra courses, as I said, that I hoped would fill in some of the information I think I need to know for life and my job."

"I think we will get along just fine. Good night, and have a safe journey home."

Totally spent both mentally and physically from the stress of meetings, questions from the executive group and working in high gear for the past two days, Ruby slept well all night.

The Call

Silently, deep in thought, Ruby rode by limo to Los Angeles International Airport. She flew home on the third day without the affirmative phrase she wanted to hear: *You're hired.* Yes, she was sure they were going to hire her; after all, they did say they would recommend her. She was on information overload. She had lots more questions swirling around in her head. She welcomed the peaceful flight home. She thought about Mr. Redwood's comments: *A college graduate. Wow! That's a real ego boost.*

The phone call Ruby had been waiting for came the next day. She answered with her most friendly voice. "Hello?"

"Hello, Ruby. Michael Brown, president of Mix and Match Cosmetics here. Would you please meet me at my office at four this afternoon?"

"Sure. I'll be there." The butterflies were back in her stomach. She was now more certain than ever that she had a new job. Surely they wouldn't invite her to the office to tell her she wasn't hired.

When Ruby arrived at the office of Mix and Match Cosmetics, her stomach was in a knot. She was full of anticipation but just couldn't let it out because she hadn't formally been made the job offer. Ruby entered the building and looked around. She was thinking, *This is where I'm going to be working. I like it.*

The receptionist asked, "How can I help you?"

"My name's Ruby Monroe. I have a four o'clock appointment with Mr. Michael Brown."

"Thank you. I'll let him know you're here." The receptionist said into the telephone, "Hi, Dana. I have a Ruby Monroe to see Mr. Brown." She hung up, looked over at Ruby and said, "Dana will be right with you."

"Thank you," was all Ruby could get out due to nerves.

Just then, Dana appeared in the doorway. "Hi, Ruby. How was your trip?"

"It was wonderful. My brain is worn out right now, but I'm fine."

They arrived at the president's office. Dana said, "Mr. Brown, your four o'clock is here."

Michael rose from his chair and walked around his desk, hand outstretched. "Hello, Ruby," he said. "Come in. Sit down."

"Thank you. That was quite the trip. They were excellent hosts as well."

"Well, the head office is sold on Ruby Monroe, unanimously. Welcome to Mix and Match Cosmetics. When can you start?"

"How about next Monday?"

"Works for me. We can chat more when you start. See you on Monday."

They shook hands, and Ruby left.

Chapter 38

Working at Mix and Match Cosmetics was better than Ruby could have ever imagined. As promised, the company sent her for training in union negotiations. She loved it and excelled at it, developing new skills and a much higher profile than she had ever experienced before. Her self-confidence was evident in her daily work and in the decisions and recommendations she made regarding the human resources implementation of policies and the collective agreement with the Steelworkers of America.

Four months later, totally out of the blue, she received a telephone call from Walter Pomp. "Hi, Ruby. How're you doing? It's Walt. I hope you didn't forget me already."

"No, Walt, how could I forget you? How are things going there?" Ruby asked. She *was* a little curious

"I would really like to make up for the negative result of our last chat," he said. "Would you consider coming back and working for us? We've fired, what did you call him? ... 'the weasel'?" They both chuckled. "We're wondering what it would take to get Ruby back to our company."

Ruby smiled. This amused her. She said, "I'm very happy to say thanks but no thanks, Walt. I have a great job now. I report to the president and I'm a member of the senior management team. As much as I hate to admit it, the weasel actually did me a favour."

"Are you sure? I have a mandate to offer you 10 percent more than your current salary there."

Ruby felt the push, noting that he was eager to fulfill a promise to his dad and CEO to lure her back to the company.

"Walt, you said Mr. Miller handled my termination poorly. I assumed you needed him because he had Labour Relations experience and I didn't." she shared.

"Sure, and that was true. We had no idea that his style of negotiation with the Autoworkers was tough, non-relenting, lock-them-out style and would totally shut down our production for two months. It played havoc with our cash flow and the bottom line as well." Walt was eating humble pie, and he knew it.

"Walt, I just completed negotiations with the Steelworkers, a really tough bunch of guys. We got the contract signed without a work stoppage and within budget. See, I can do it. If only you had given me a chance," she said, gloating a bit. *Wow! My ego just got bigger. I might have trouble getting my fat head through the doorway.*

"Congratulations, Ruby," said Walt. "That saying is true: you don't appreciate who you have until they're gone. Mix and Match's gain is our loss. I'm sorry for us, as I think you would have been a much better fit in this environment." He waited, hoping she would be curious enough to come for an interview. When Walt heard nothing coming back from Ruby, he said, "Don't be a stranger. Good luck, Ruby. You deserve your good fortune. Bye for now."

"Thanks for the ego boost, Walt. Bye," she said with a Cheshire cat grin. Not to be nasty, but she hoped Walt could hear it in her tone.

Ruby blossomed at Mix and Match Cosmetics. She loved the glamour, the constant shows and the product introductions. As a senior manager of the company, she was invited to high-fashion promotional events, all expenses paid. She traveled to Hollywood for strategic planning meetings with the top HR and labour relations people. This was her dream job.

Everything is perfect, she thought. *I'm secure financially and socially. Nothing can go wrong now.*

Chapter 39

1981: More Changes

Eighteen months into their relationship, during one of his visits, George dropped a bomb in the middle of a romantic dinner. He said, "I think I'm ready to make a commitment to marriage again."

Ruby drew in a lungful of air. She wasn't sure what he meant by that. She didn't want to get married; she was having too much fun. *After being physically and psychologically beaten and abused for more than twenty years, I'm not prepared to give up my freedom just yet.*

She felt a slight panic as questions rushed through her mind. *Is he tired of me? Is he seeing someone else? Maybe he just wants to move on.*

George continued, "I would also like to have another child."

Bang! Ouch! It felt like a one-two punch in the stomach, and it knocked the wind out of her. *Deep down, I always knew this day would come,* she realized. *Pregnancy definitely is not something I want to consider. I already have children. Been there, done that, as the saying goes.*

He noticed her silence and complete withdrawal. "Ruby, I knew this was a very risky thing to say, but I have always been honest with you. I do understand that this is not the time for more change in your life."

"You can say that again," she agreed. "Everything in my life has been in constant flux for a couple of years now."

An odd silence hung over them. Together, they cleared up the dinner dishes and put them in the dishwasher. They both felt the tension in the room. Neither one spoke for quite some time.

Finally, George, holding the wine bottle, asked, "Ruby, would you like more wine?"

She responded in a monotone voice, "Sure. That sounds good." It was apparent that she was deep in thought and not ready to talk about George's bold statement.

He asked, "Another glass for you George? Sure, I think I will." This was his attempt to lighten up the mood. "Ruby, can we talk?" he said next. "I would really like to temper my comments. I want you to know that I'm not seeing anyone else, nor do I at this time have any desire to see another person. You are great for me. We are great together."

They took their wine to bed, as had become their habit. They liked to drink their wine with their post-coital pillow talk. Their lovemaking had become gentle and patient, while still very passionate. It had become much more about loving each other and giving each other pleasure. Unlike in the beginning, it was more than just plain crazy desperate passionate sex.

They gently kissed all of their arousal spots, each reaching a climax during oral stimulation. Then, as the icing on the cake, the cherry on top, came the penetration of his beautiful engorged cock. She had become very fond of his penis for the absolute exceptional sensual pleasure she experienced. George was now more familiar with Ruby's most erotic zones and how to give her the greatest mind-blowing earth-shattering orgasms. He always watched for her familiar smile to appear when she was ready, and he did his best to bestow a *Merry Christmas my darling*.

Ruby still loved her orgasms, even with the more familiar George. Her orgasms continued to lift her mind, body and soul up—up—up like a surfer gliding to the top of a huge wave. As usual, it took her breath away. Holding her breath, she waited to reach the top, soon now—soon—almost there, and then there was the explosion that she said felt like the earth moved under her and sent her to the most amazing heights, with that special spot pulsating. She felt it through her whole body. Each and every time, this sensation was so strong she groaned as it lifted her head off the pillow. Her body relaxed, and slowly, ever so slowly, she floated back to reality with the warmest spectacular glow inside and out. She was left huffing and puffing, trying to catch her breath while she enjoyed the afterglow. She smiled at George and said, "Xmas didn't disappoint this time or ever."

They cuddled, enjoying the great totally spent feelings, and then they fell into a restful and relaxed sleep in each other's arms.

Chapter 40
Life Changing Decision

Ruby knew she must make a decision and very soon. There was no way she wanted to become pregnant. She didn't want to deprive George of having children either; after all, he was ten years younger than her and in his prime reproductive years.

She made an appointment with her gynaecologist, and he agreed to perform a tubal litigation. He didn't think it was wise for her to become pregnant at her age, especially as a dating single gal. His nurse booked the surgery and hospital stay. Ruby would need to remain in the hospital for one day and night as an in-patient, as there would be no one at home to watch her for the first twenty-four hours following surgery.

That evening, over dinner, she managed to gather the courage to tell George of her decision. "I made an appointment and saw my gynaecologist today." She explained her dilemma. "George, I do love you, and I have enjoyed every second of our relationship. You have been good for me. I feel that after my divorce, because you were there to catch me, I didn't falter. There is only one thing that I won't do for you: I cannot give you a child. This is unfair, I know, as you are a good, loving, kind and thoughtful father. You deserve complete fulfillment in your life. Maybe that special someone will come along for you to love, and the two of you can make babies."

George got up from the table and came to her, offering a huge bear hug. "I didn't say I was leaving. I just wanted to be upfront and honest with you, because this has been the strength of our relationship."

Ruby quoted the advice that Doctor Mitchell had given her. "He said it was not a good idea to get pregnant once you turn 40, mainly due to the possibility of birth defects. Statistics are not on my side for delivering a healthy baby. He suggested that I have this surgery, a tubal ligation, which would prevent me from getting pregnant. It's not reversible, so he suggested that I think about the surgery for a few days. I have, and I plan to go ahead with the procedure."

"That's my mature, practical lady."

"George, I need to do this. I'm sorry, but I just don't want to risk getting pregnant." Ruby had no doubt this was the right decision for her.

They both knew this choice would make a huge difference in their relationship and impact its future. Actually, this pronouncement was the beginning of the end of their support and therapy together.

"Ruby, I really do understand," he said. Then he added, "This is the first time our age disparity has ever been an issue. I do appreciate and understand why you've made the decision you have and the major impact it will have on our relationship. Please understand mine."

Tears were streaming down her cheeks as she said, "George, I do understand, and I believe it is the right decision for you. Please know that I do care very deeply and even love you on so many levels, but I must do this. I didn't come to this decision lightly, and I am adamant that this is the right choice for me. I hope you understand and can respect my decision also. I'm so sorry."

By the look on his face, she knew he understood. Neither one ever put it into words, but they knew that being there for each other and supporting each other was the reason they had hooked up in the beginning. Now it was time for both of them to move on. This was their fork in the road.

George and Ruby continued their relationship, more off than on, for about six more months. Their love affair had lasted almost two wonderful years, but then he wanted more. They equally cherished having the other in their life and the great times they shared. Both had healed, but as scary as it was, it was time to venture out into the world and find a life mate.

A few months later, Ruby found her life mate on the squash courts. They were on the same team. A few days before Christmas, the teams were having a few beers after a tough championship match. One of her teammates, Paul, starting talking to her and then asked what she was doing for Christmas. She told him she was busy but not on Christmas Eve. So their first date was a Christmas Eve church service. Paul also invited her to a party at his friend Bob's place on Boxing Day.

Paul was a very lanky guy at 6 feet 4 inches, tall enough to be a basketball player, with a very muscular body from playing squash almost every day. Ruby liked his mild-mannered demeanour and his kindness toward her. Like her, he had an undeniable love of animals. Paul was a smart business person who was respected by his clients, competitors and regulators. Ruby felt his love every day. He was a fun travel companion, as his masters degree was in geography.

Paul pledged his love for Ruby daily, as he loved her deeply. His personality forbade him from using violence to settle differences; he deemed it unacceptable, regardless of who he dealt with or was fighting against.

Epilogue

She was so thankful to have had George as a support person. He'd helped her heal and build back her battered self-esteem. This was the main reason she now had the poise and confidence to go out into the world and help others—maybe even to be the bold feminist she had become.

George and Ruby ended as fond platonic friends. They met for drinks, at first every week, then once a month, then less and less until they no longer needed to share their lives with each other. Both had found someone to love and fill that void in a more permanent way.

She loved Jason's parents and visited them frequently, long after the divorce. They never knew about Jason's cruel and abusive behaviour. His mother, a beautiful lady, would have been mortified. Ruby didn't tell them out of love and respect; they were good people. His mother did ask her several times what happened to cause her to divorce Jason; naturally, she was curious. Ruby chose to sugar-coat her response. Ruby stayed friends with her mother-in-law and visited her frequently, later with Paul, until she died at age 91.

I'm free and doing just fine, thought Ruby. *Most of the psychological wounds have healed or are healing. There is only one faint lingering question: Why did I put up with the abuse, adultery and fear for so long? I'm a strong person in spite of those years. I'm married to a kind and loving man. I have wonderful children and a great job—everything anyone could want—thanks to George and everyone in my life, past, present and future.*

Through her very strong memories, Ruby is frequently reminded of her strength, determination and love. She no longer hurts from the abuse, physically or mentally. There are no lingering doubts about the depth of her strength and the guts it took to pull herself up and out of the abusive environment. She often feared for her life and the safety of herself and her children over twenty-plus years of that marriage. She was a far stronger person now. The latter part of her story consisted of good memories that lasted for many, many years. Finally putting this memoir on paper has been the best therapy and has put everything in perspective.

Ruby had come a long way, and she had no interest in looking back. There was nothing back there for her.

>Scars remind us where we've been.
>They don't need to dictate where we're going.
>—unknown

Printed in the United States
By Bookmasters